"Hey, hey, what's this?"

Leo took her ███████████████ ds.

She couldn'█████████████████
do this to m█████████████ him.
I gave you ev████████████

He stroked her ███ and, speaking softly,
gently, said, "I know I haven't been much
of a husband lately, but the past three
weeks have been…difficult. My brother's
death has caused all sorts of problems,
problems too complex and numerous to
explain. Suffice to say I've sorted them
out now."

Brooke listened to this subtly worded
confession without a shred of reassurance
or forgiveness. How smooth he was, she
realized. How clever. How *patronizing!*
"I probably haven't told you this often
enough," he went on, bending to press
his lips into her hair, "but I *do* love you,
Brooke…."

Brooke stopped breathing. How could
words so longed for strike like daggers
into her heart? For she knew who her
husband really loved….

Miranda Lee

MARRIAGE IN PERIL

ITALIAN HUSBANDS

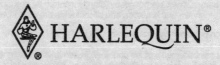

HARLEQUIN®

TORONTO • NEW YORK • LONDON
AMSTERDAM • PARIS • SYDNEY • HAMBURG
STOCKHOLM • ATHENS • TOKYO • MILAN • MADRID
PRAGUE • WARSAW • BUDAPEST • AUCKLAND

ISBN 0-373-12326-4

MARRIAGE IN PERIL

First North American Publication 2003.

This edition published by arrangement with Harlequin Books S.A.

® and TM are trademarks of the publisher. Trademarks indicated with
® are registered in the United States Patent and Trademark Office, the
Canadian Trade Marks Office and in other countries.

Visit us at www.eHarlequin.com

Printed in U.S.A.

PROLOGUE

BROOKE steeled herself for her mother's reaction to her news. It wouldn't be good. But there again, she reminded herself ruefully, her mother never approved of any of her decisions.

Not that Brooke was in the habit of being all that assertive. She'd only crossed her mother's will a few times in her twenty-two years, and most of those had been secret transgressions, like reading with a torch under the bedclothes at night. And putting on lipstick the moment she turned the corner on her way to school.

Her only major openly defiant decisions had been taking an apprenticeship in the hospitality industry with a large Sydney hotel rather than doing law at university, followed by her move out of home last year to live by herself in a small bedsit at Bondi.

But neither of those decisions had been as mammoth as planning to marry at a register office ceremony tomorrow morning, *without* breathing a word to her mother about either her husband-to-be or the marriage till this very moment.

Tension built within Brooke while she waited for her mother to say something. But Phyllis Freeman just sat there at the green garden table, smoking. Silent.

The silent treatment was not a tactic her mother adopted very often. She was a highly intelligent and assertive woman, with a sharp mind and an even sharper tongue, who used argument and ruthless logic to get her way. She had definite ideas about everything, but especially the role and rights of the modern woman.

A lawyer who specialised in discrimination cases, Phyllis was an expert in arguing the feminist cause. At forty-two, and with two divorces behind her, she had become a dedicated man-hater, plus the most difficult of mothers.

Brooke had no idea why she loved her. The woman was impossible. She'd driven away two good husbands, and driven Brooke herself to distraction ever since she'd started dating. No boyfriend had ever found favour with Phyllis Freeman. There'd always been something wrong with them.

No wonder when Brooke had met Leo she'd never brought him home to meet her mother. Brooke hadn't wanted to risk spoiling what she knew was the greatest love of her life.

But things had progressed beyond that now—now her mother had to be acquainted with the facts. Her marriage to Leo was about to become a *fait accompli*.

Brook had toyed with the idea of not telling her mother till *after* the event, but had decided that would be too cruel. At the moment, however, she thought it might have been the lesser of two evils.

Brooke's stomach tightened as she watched her mother finally stab out her cigarette in the ceramic ashtray and look up at her with icy blue eyes.

'Was marriage your idea, Brooke?' she asked coldly. 'Or his?'

'His, actually,' Brooke took pleasure in announcing. She'd been over the moon when Leo had proposed straight away on knowing about the baby. Because then she'd known he really loved her, and wasn't just out for a good time.

Her mother had always said actions spoke louder than words. Well, marriage equated with love and commitment in Brooke's mind. It wasn't just her so-called beautiful face and body Leo wanted—something her mother had always gone to great pains to point out about her previous boyfriends.

Brooke wondered if that was what her mother had believed about herself in the past. That the men in her life had been blinded by her looks, that none had ever really loved Phyllis the person. As a young woman Phyllis had been a stunner, with long blonde hair, creamy skin, big blue eyes, full, pouty lips and a body just made for sin. Brooke was often told she was the spitting image of her mother at the same age.

The years, however, had wrought many changes in Phyllis Freeman. Chain-smoking had aged her skin and bitterness had thinned her mouth. Her once lovely long blonde hair was now cut ruthlessly short and going grey at the roots. A dedicated feminist, Brooke's mother never went to the hairdresser's, or wore make-up. She was too thin as well, in Brooke's opinion, living on cigarettes and coffee.

Brooke worried about her mother's health.

'I suppose you refused to consider an abortion,' Phyllis scorned, 'being the hopeless romantic you are.'

Brooke almost hated her at that moment. 'I didn't consider it for a moment,' she said indignantly. 'I love Leo, Mum. With all my heart.'

'I have no doubt you do, darling,' Phyllis returned,

though her eyes remained cynical. 'Why else would an intelligent girl sleep with a man without using protection unless she was in love? But why did he, I wonder?' she mused.

Brooke refused to say a word on *that* subject. No way was she going to admit to being so instantly besotted with Leo that she'd been quite shameless in her swift surrender to his impassioned pursuit of her. Not to mention totally reckless. She'd stupidly deceived him in matters of contraception that first night because she hadn't wanted him to stop, even for a second, and she had genuinely thought it was a safe time. The same thing had applied each night over the following week.

But it hadn't been safe at all. When her period hadn't arrived at the end of that first marvellous week, she hadn't panicked. But when it hadn't made an appearance by the end of another fortnight, and a pregnancy test had confirmed she was going to have a baby, Brooke had been too afraid to confess everything, so she'd pretended that she'd forgotten to take the pill on one of those first tempestuous nights together. At the time she hadn't been trying to trap Leo into marriage. She'd just been unbelievably stupid!

But he'd been so wonderful when she'd confessed her pregnant state. And not at all angry. Comforting and caring when she'd cried. Solid and strong when she'd said she didn't know what to do.

'Don't worry, *mi micetta*,' he'd murmured soothingly as he held her close. He always called her that. It meant little kitten. He said she was like a kitten after they'd made love, practically purring as he stroked her as he liked to do afterwards. 'We'll get married as soon as it can be arranged. But not a big wedding. And no honeymoon, I'm afraid. I do not have time for that right now.'

Only occasionally did she feel a stab of guilt over deceiving Leo, but never when in his arms, never when he called her his *micetta*.

She felt a bit guilty now. Not over Leo. Over her mother. She was probably very hurt by being kept in the dark like this.

But Brooke refused to apologise. Or back down. Once you took a backward step with Phyllis Freeman she went for the jugular.

'So what does your husband-to-be do for a living?' her mother asked abruptly.

'He's a businessman. His family company imports Italian goods into countries all over the world. Leo's in the process of opening an office and warehouse here in Sydney.'

'How enterprising of him,' Phyllis drawled. 'And where did you meet this…Leo? He doesn't sound like your usual style of boyfriend.'

'He's been living in a suite at the Majestic till he can buy a house,' Brooke said, and watched that information sink in.

The Majestic was one of Sydney's most expensive hotels, a lavish, luxurious concern which overlooked the Harbour and the Opera House, and boasted pop stars and presidents amongst its clientele. Brooke had been working on the main desk for just over six months, and it had been there, on a warm summer evening back in February, just over two months ago, that she'd looked up from the computer and straight into Leo's incredibly sexy black eyes.

'So what's his full name?' Phyllis asked sourly. 'This fine, successful businessman called Leo, who's impregnated my daughter but doesn't have the courage to face me himself.'

'He *did* want to face you,' Brooke defended. 'It's me who insisted on coming in alone first.'

'Really?'

'Yes. Really. His full name is Leonardo Giuseppe Parini,' she said proudly, thinking it was a wonderful name, with a wonderful heritage. Leo had told her his family could trace its ancestors back for generations. In the eighteenth century one of his forefathers had been a famous poet.

'He's *Italian*?' Phyllis exclaimed, horrified.

Brooke was taken aback by her mother's reaction. 'Well…yes. He was born in Milan. But he speaks English perfectly,' she hurried on, full of pride and praise for her handsome and clever husband-to-be. 'He travelled a lot with his parents as a child. And he studied business at Harvard. He spent a few years working in New York, then London and Paris. And now he's here in Sydney. He hardly has any accent at all.' Just enough to be very, very sexy.

'His accent isn't the problem, Brooke,' her mother bit out. 'Accent or no accent, he's a born and bred Italian.'

'What's the problem with that?'

'At least I now understand why he's marrying you,' her mother muttered. 'An Australian man would probably have run a mile. Italian men have this *thing* about their offspring, especially sons. I hope you realise, Brooke, how Italians treat their wives once a wedding ring is on their finger and they have them under lock and key at home. Like second-class citizens. Chattels. Italian wives are never partners. Just possessions and producers of children.'

'Leo's not like that!' Brooke defended, her face instantly hot with resentment and fury. Trust her mother to start criticising before she'd even met the man. 'And you're wrong about Italian men. That's an ignorant and very offensive opinion!'

Why, her best friend in high school had been Italian, and her father had been a wonderful man. Brooke had loved going over to Antonia's house. It had been so much warmer than her own. No tension or arguments. Just a whole lot of warmth, and closeness, and love.

'Don't be ridiculous,' Phyllis snapped. 'All men are like that, given the opportunity. But chauvinism is *bred* into Italian men. They think they're gods within their own family circles and demand to be treated as such, no questions asked. Italian women seem to be able to cope. They're brought up with different values and expectations. But you're not Italian, Brooke. You're Australian. You're also *my* daughter. There's more of me in you than you realise, whether you admit it or not. He'll make you miserable. You mark my words.'

'You're wrong!' Brooke lashed back. 'He won't make me miserable because I won't make *him* miserable. And I'm *not* like you. Not in any way. In my eyes, Leo *is* a god. Nothing is too good for him. I'm never going to drive him away like you did Dad, with your constant arguing and criticising. No wonder he left you. I'm going to give my husband whatever he wants. I'm going to be there for him whenever he needs me.'

'Become a doormat, you mean.'

'Not a doormat. A wife!'

'Same thing, in some men's eyes.'

Brooke shook her head in despair and frustration. 'You have no idea how to make a man happy. You never did.'

'Not if it meant suppressing every thought, wish and opinion in my head! You're an intelligent girl, Brooke. And you're quite stubborn and wilful in your own way. If you think squashing everything *you* are will bring you lasting happiness, then you're in for a shock one day.'

Brooke said nothing, gritted her teeth and just counted to ten. 'Are you going to come to my wedding or not?'

'Would it make any difference?'

Brooke sighed a weary sigh. 'Of course it would make a difference. I want you there at my wedding. You're my mother.'

'Then I'll be there, I suppose. Just like I'll be there to pick up the pieces when the honeymoon is over. And it will be over one day, Brooke. I hope you realise that.'

'Leo and I are *never* getting a divorce, no matter what!'

'You say that now,' Phyllis said as she lit up another cigarette. 'I wonder what you might say in five years' time.'

'The answer will be the same.'

'I truly hope so, darling. Now…' She dragged deeply on the cigarette and let it out slowly. 'Am I going to meet this handsome Italian of yours or not?' The corner of her mouth lifted in a knowing little smirk. 'He *is* handsome, I presume? Never known you to go out with an ugly bloke. Not you, Brooke.'

Brooke's chin lifted. 'He's *very* handsome.'

'Then go get him. I'm beginning to be just a little bit curious about Leonardo Giuseppe Parini.'

Brooke was the one smiling when she led Leo back into her mother's presence, her arms linked tightly around his. For she knew her lover of two months and imminent husband-to-be wasn't just handsome. He was simply magnificent. In every way.

A mature and sophisticated thirty-two, he was tall for an Italian, at six foot two, with an elegant but well-shaped body and a face Valentino would have envied. It combined the best of all things Latin, with slightly hooded and absolutely riveting black eyes, a classic nose and a highly sensual mouth. His hair was even blacker than his eyes, its glossy thickness giving added style and shape to its up-to-date fashion of being cut quite short. Brooke thought him the most handsome man she'd ever seen.

But it was his presentation which really impressed. His utter perfection in matters of dress and grooming. His coolly confident bearing. His grace of movement.

Brooke's smile broadened as she watched her mother's eyes widen and her mouth fall rather inelegantly open.

'This is Leo, Mum,' Brooke said smugly, and ran a possessive hand down his sleekly suited arm.

Phyllis Freeman was rendered totally speechless for the first time in her life.

CHAPTER ONE

Italy…five years later.

BROOKE stretched out on top of the bed and tried to go to sleep, as everyone else was doing that warm, sultry afternoon. But it was impossible. She'd never been a sleeper during the day. On top of that, she was feeling restless and edgy.

Her gaze drifted agitatedly around the huge and very lavish bedroom, then up at the ornate frescoed ceiling and the elaborate crystal and gold chandelier which hung from its centre.

This was the main guest room, where she and Leo always stayed during their annual visit to the Parini family villa on Lake Como.

'Only the best for my son and his lovely wife,' his mother had said the first time Leo had brought Brooke and their baby son home, just on four years ago.

Brooke sighed at the memory of that first visit, and their subsequent yearly visits. What heaven they always were! With an English-speaking Italian girl to help mind the children, and more time to relax, it was almost like being on a honeymoon each year—the one they'd never had.

Their sex life had always been good—fantastic to start with!—and it was still pretty good. Leo would probably say it was *very* good. But Leo wasn't a stay-at-home mother with two children under five.

Many was the night Brooke just didn't feel like sex.

But she never refused Leo, not unless she was really sick. Of course, that meant faking an orgasm every once in a while. But she did it. For him.

Brooke frowned at the thought she'd been doing that quite a bit lately.

During their Italian stays, however, faking anything was never required. No longer tired from continuous child-minding, Brooke was more easily put in the mood. As for Leo…he would become practically insatiable, wanting her not just at night but during the day as well.

Four years ago, when he'd first suggested they take an afternoon nap at the same time as Alessandro was sleeping—he'd been their only child back then—she'd thought he'd gone crazy. The idea of Leo having an afternoon nap had been just plain ridiculous. The man was a dynamo, needing very little sleep at the best of times.

But he'd insisted, despite her blank look, and she'd finally twigged—courtesy of the knowing gleam in Leo's father's eyes. She'd blushed madly as Leo had practically dragged her up to the bedroom for a couple of hours' torrid lovemaking.

Brooke had been a bit stunned at first. Leo hadn't made love to her like that since before they were married. He'd been gentle and considerate during her whole pregnancy, and hadn't complained at all during the six weeks after Alessandro's birth when the doctor had vetoed any sex. Even when Leo had been given the green light he'd still been tender with her, which she'd appreciated. She'd had stitches and been pretty sore and sorry for herself for a while. He'd also seemed to appreciate the fact she was tired most of the time during Alessandro's first six months. Far too tired for lovemaking marathons.

But that afternoon, although not rough with her, he'd been incredibly demanding. Whilst Brooke had found everything slightly shocking in broad daylight—plus in his parents' house—it *had* been exciting, and she hadn't needed dragging upstairs the next day. Or any day afterwards.

Claudia had been born eight and a half months after their return to Sydney.

But this visit was entirely different in every way. It wasn't their annual holiday which had brought them to Como a little earlier than usual this year, but a funeral. Leo's only sibling, Lorenzo, had been killed in a car accident, losing control of his prized Ferrari on one of the hairpin bends around the lake and crashing to a watery death.

Fortunately, Lorenzo's wife, Francesca, had not been in the car at the time, although maybe she didn't think she was fortunate. The poor woman had been almost comatose with grief at the funeral, unable to function at all. With Francesca's own parents long dead, Leo's mum and dad had brought Lorenzo's widow home to the villa for some tender loving care, and everyone had done their best to offer comfort, despite their own unhappiness.

But it was difficult to know what to say to her. Brooke thought it was a shame the marriage had never produced children. Children would have given Francesca something to live for.

Brooke had tried to talk to her on one occasion, but the woman had just burst into tears and run back to her room, where she'd stayed for the rest of the day. Brooke had felt terrible, and had told Leo's mum about it. Sophia had just patted her hand and smiled a sad smile, telling her not to worry, it wasn't her fault. Francesca was just being Francesca.

Brooke knew exactly what she meant. Francesca was a weak kind of woman, in her opinion. Very beautiful in a dark-eyed, lush-figured way. But she never said much, or exuded much personality.

Not that Brooke had been in their company all that often over their four-year acquaintance. Just the occasional family dinner party, sometimes here at the villa, and sometimes in Lorenzo's plush apartment in Milan.

Francesca would sit silently beside her husband on such occasions, her eyes darting nervously to him all the time, as though waiting to be told what to do, or say. Brooke could never work out if she adored the man or was afraid of him.

Two years older than Leonardo, Lorenzo had been a handsome and charming man on the surface, but Brooke hadn't been able to stand him. He'd given her the creeps. Once, during a party at his place, she'd gone to the powder room. She'd been in there, washing her hands, when he'd come in unexpectedly and made the most disgusting suggestion. She'd been so shocked she hadn't known what to do, except run out of the room and hurry back downstairs.

She hadn't told Leo about the incident. No way.

Brooke wasn't stupid, and she'd sensed there was some angst between the two brothers. They'd been civil on the surface, but nothing more. Brooke had got the impression Leo didn't like his brother's wife much, either, an opinion reinforced by his coldly indifferent stance when Francesca had suddenly upped and gone back to Milan a week ago. To be by herself, she'd said. Everyone had objected, thinking it a potentially dangerous idea; everyone except Leo.

To be honest, Brooke hadn't really been sorry to see Francesca go. Her presence had hung like a pall over the house, bringing tensions she didn't quite understand, not being one of the family.

Leo was actually the lucky one, in her opinion, since he was out of the house most days. He'd been driving back and forth to the Milan office during the working week, going through his brother's desk and sorting out who was going to take charge there now. Brooke had worried his father might ask him to come back and do the job Lorenzo had been doing—Giuseppe had retired with heart problems the previous year—but this hadn't eventuated, thank God.

She was grateful for that, but beginning to resent the amount of time Leo was spending away from her and the children. This past week, the situation had worsened, with her husband getting home later and later each night. After a quick supper and a shower, he would fall into bed, too tired to make love, a most unusual situation for Leo.

If there was one thing Brooke could rely upon with her husband, it was the unfailing regularity of his need for sex. Yet he hadn't laid a hand on her since the funeral, almost three weeks ago.

Brooke was beginning to miss the feelings of love and intimacy Leo's lovemaking always left her with, even when she was faking things. Every woman liked to be wanted that way.

Sighing, Brooke swung her feet over the side of the bed and stood up. Flicking her long fair hair back over her shoulder, she picked up the novel she kept by the bed and padded across the huge Persian rug towards the sliding glass doors which led out onto the balcony. Once outside, in the cooler air, she settled herself in one of the comfy deckchairs and opened her book at the page she'd reached the previous night.

After several minutes scanning the page without a single word sinking in, Brooke closed the book and just sat there, doing her best to relax and enjoy a view coveted the world over.

The first time she'd seen Lake Como she'd been wide-eyed over the scenic beauty of the mountains rising up from the crystalline lake; at the magnificence of the huge villas clinging to the hillsides; at the number of luxury yachts in the water, plus the all-round postcard perfection of the place.

She'd been even more wide-eyed when Leo had pulled up outside his family's summer home.

The Parini villa was not as large as some, but larger than most, showing evidence of the family's long-held wealth. The house had been built in the late eighteenth century, then added to and renovated several times since. Multi-levelled, it had acres of marble flooring, more bedrooms than Brooke could count, huge open-plan living areas, several very formal entertaining rooms, expansive terracotta terraces, a solar-heated swimming pool, and perfectly manicured lawns which sloped down to a private dock where three boats were moored. A speed boat, a cruiser and a racing yacht. Inside, monumental paintings filled the walls, and everywhere there were the most incredible antiques.

Brooke had worried over the years that her boisterous and mischievous son might ruin or break something, but oddly he hadn't, as though he recognised that these treasures were his to inherit one day and had to be preserved.

Although half-Australian, Alessandro was a very Italian child. Openly affectionate, noisy and demanding, he was far too good-looking for his own good, with his father's dark hair and eyes.

Claudia was dark-haired and dark-eyed too, and very pretty, but much quieter and delightfully amenable, content to follow her mother around, or just to play with her dolls. Her brother had to be always on the move, always doing something. Since the age of two, he'd refused to take no for an answer.

Like father like son, Brooke thought ruefully.

Which brought her thoughts back to Leo. Her darling Leo, whom she still adored but who was not the easiest man to live with, she'd found. He really did like his way in everything. Many were the times she'd been tempted to argue with him, to try to get *her* way for once, but she never had.

Except once…when Claudia was born.

Brooke had wanted to call her daughter Chloe. She'd also wanted to call Alessandro Alexander, but had

given in when Leo had explained that the heir to the
Parini fortune should have an Italian name.

Brooke hadn't really minded, since Alessandro
wasn't so different from Alexander. But when she'd
had a daughter, she'd expected to be able to choose the
name *she* wanted. Not so, she had soon found out. Leo
had been adamant about Claudia, then angry when
Brooke had argued with him. More angry than she had
ever seen him.

'I am the head of this family,' he'd pronounced dog-
matically. 'What I say goes!'

For a split second, Brooke had been overwhelmed
by a deep, violent anger of her own. *You're just like
my mother said,* she'd almost thrown at him.

Thinking of her mother, however, had forced her to
get a grip on herself. You don't want to end up like
her, do you? Bitter and twisted and lonely. It's only a
name, after all. What's in a name? It's not worth getting a divorce over.

So, once again, she'd given in.

But it still hurt a little; his not seeing her point of
view on something that was important to her; his not
meeting her halfway.

Her mother had warned her she would become a
doormat. Well, maybe she had in a way, she conceded.
But she was a happy and contented doormat. Most of
the time.

A telephone ringing somewhere downstairs had her
rising from the depths of the deckchair, only to sink
down again when it was swiftly answered.

Determinedly, Brooke picked up her book again, and
was doing her best to become absorbed in the story

when a voice drifted up from the terrace below. It was Leo's mother. Despite her speaking in Italian, Brooke understood every word.

She'd always been good at languages, and had studied Latin and Japanese at school. After her marriage to Leo, Brooke had made the effort to learn Italian, picking it up quickly from tapes and books, then practising it with Leo in the evenings, plus every time she visited his family. She had no trouble following the conversation below.

'There you are, Giuseppe,' Sophia said. 'I see you couldn't sleep, either. That was Leonardo on the phone.'

Brooke's ears immediately pricked.

'Anything wrong?' came Giuseppe's reply.

'He's going to be late again. Doesn't want us to keep any dinner for him this time.'

Brooke groaned. Just when she'd been wanting him to come home a bit earlier.

'So?' Giuseppe said with a shrug in his voice. 'Why the worried frown?'

'If he has so much work on his plate, Giuseppe, why didn't he ask you to go in with him? It's not as though you couldn't spend a few hours in the office here and there.'

'I offered, woman, but he refused. Told me one death in the family was enough for this year. But you're right. He *did* look tired last night. I'll insist on joining him tomorrow.'

'Tomorrow might be too late, Giuseppe.'

'Too late for what?'

'I don't think he's *in* the office today…' Sophia said in more hushed tones.

Brooke leant forward in her chair.

'…I think he's with Francesca.'

Brooke's heart lurched.

'What?' Giuseppe exploded. 'Don't be ridiculous, woman! Leonardo is not that type of man. He would never be unfaithful to that lovely little wife of his. Never!'

Brooke was glad she was sitting down. If she hadn't been, she might have fallen down.

'Not normally, Giuseppe,' she heard Sophia say. 'But these are not normal circumstances. Leonardo was in love with Francesca long before Brooke came into his life. He never got over Lorenzo stealing Francesca away from him. He might have pretended to, but I know differently. I'm his mother.'

'For pity's sake, that was years ago!'

'Maybe, but Leonardo is not a fickle man. I always knew that when he fell in love it would be for life.'

'Leonardo loves his *wife*!' his father defended, outrage in his voice.

'Has he said as much to you?'

An increasingly stricken Brooke strained forward further, waiting to hear Leo's father say firmly, *Yes, of course. Many times!*

'Men don't talk about things like that, woman. But it's as obvious as the nose on my face.'

Sophia sighed. 'I've no doubt he *does* love Brooke, in a fashion. She's a very beautiful girl. And incredibly sweet. But he was *in love* with Francesca. I will never forget the way he looked at her on the night of their engagement party, with such hunger in his eyes. To find her in bed that same night with his brother must have nearly killed him.'

On the balcony above Brooke was reeling from shock after shock. Leo...*her* Leo, in love with Francesca? Her husband, once *engaged* to his brother's wife? Francesca choosing *Lorenzo* over Leo?

'Unfortunately,' Sophia went on with another sigh, 'Leonardo handled Francesca the wrong way back then, playing the gentleman with her. He thought respecting her virginity was the right thing to do. But he was wrong. Lorenzo, to my eternal dismay, had no respect for anything, or anyone. He simply took what he wanted, and silly, shy, naive Francesca was swept away by his decadent wickedness.'

'You're talking nonsense, woman! Lorenzo was not wicked, just weak in matters of the flesh. If he was truly wicked, he would not have married the girl. Yes, they did wrong, but they couldn't help themselves. They fell madly in love at first sight. Lorenzo told me so himself. He was very sorry he hurt Leonardo, but Francesca obviously didn't really love the boy. Lorenzo said she was only marrying his brother because he was kind, and she was so lonely after her father's recent death. As soon as Leonardo understood that, any feelings he had for the girl died a natural death.'

'If he no longer cared for Francesca,' Sophia scorned, 'then why did he run off to Australia? And why didn't he return for his brother's wedding?'

'He didn't run off to Australia. I *sent* him there! As for not returning for the wedding, give the man some leeway, woman. He has his pride. He did right to stay away.'

'Perhaps so. But I don't think he's staying away now. With Lorenzo dead, Leonardo finally has the opportunity to have what he foolishly denied himself back then. Francesca, in *his* bed.'

'I don't believe a son of mine would dishonour the family name in this way.'

'Why not?' Sophia said, her voice becoming hard. 'Your other son did. Often.'

'Lorenzo may have strayed once or twice. But he was a handsome man, and women threw themselves at him in a shameless fashion. It's unfortunate Francesca never had children. Children keep a man at home, and loyal. But let us talk of Lorenzo no more. The boy is dead. It is not right to speak badly of the dead. And you are wrong about Leonardo. Now, I want to hear no more about this matter.'

'Turning a blind eye will not solve this situation, husband mine,' Sophia said sternly.

'If what you say is true, then turning a blind eye is the *only* answer,' Giuseppe refuted. 'If Leo is fool enough to be having an affair with Francesca, he'll soon get her out of his system and realise there's just as good to be had at home. If I'm any judge, I'd say *better*! Leonardo and his family fly back to Sydney in two more days. Be patient and say nothing. The problem will pass.'

'Maybe you're right. But two days can be a long time...'

CHAPTER TWO

SOMEHOW Brooke made her way back into the bedroom without alerting the couple on the terrace below, there to collapse onto the gold silk quilt. Both her hands lifted to cover her eyes, as though by blocking out the light she could somehow block out the horror of what she'd just heard.

Leo, in love with *Francesca*! Leo, once *engaged* to his brother's widow! Leo, not at the office, but spending time with his lost love…

It seemed unbelievable, and yet it explained so much. The fact Leo had never actually said he loved *her*. Not *ever*! He'd used other endearments, other phrases. Adoration. Desire. Need. But never love.

And then there was his oddly cold behaviour around Francesca. Not dislike or indifference, as she'd imagined. But the other side of love.

Oh, God…

The pain wasn't just emotional. It was brutally physical. A vice clamped around her heart, pressing down till she simply couldn't breathe!

Gasping for air, Brooke struggled off the bed and into the bathroom, where she splashed some cold water over her face, then sucked in great gulps of oxygen before straightening. The distressed face staring back at her in the vanity mirror was hardly recognisable. Chalk-white, with huge, hurt blue eyes and an uncontrollably quivering chin. When tears blurred her vision her eyes dropped and her shoulders sagged. She had to clutch at the marble vanity-top to stop herself from sinking to the floor.

Dear Lord, *what* was she going to do?

Suddenly, and perversely, she wanted her mother.

Yet her mother was the last person she could tell any of this to. She would just say, *I told you so!* in that scoffing, scornful way of hers.

Brooke could not help thinking that it was almost five years since her mother had prophesied Leo would make her miserable. Next week was their fifth wedding anniversary. And she'd been right!

Or had she?

What if Giuseppe was right and Sophia was wrong? What if Leo *wasn't* still in love with Francesca, let alone spending today—or any other day—with her? What if he didn't give a damn about his brother's wife, and hadn't since she'd betrayed his love with his brother?

Brooke's heart clung to this desperate hope.

It was possible, wasn't it? Okay, so Leo *hadn't* proclaimed his undying love for her. But in the five years she'd known him he'd never given a hint that he was unhappy, or pining for another woman. He'd always seemed very happy to come home to *her* every night, and very satisfied with their life together, especially their sex life.

Till this last three weeks, that was, she conceded, with a sickening twist in her stomach. Leo hadn't been himself in that department since coming home for Lorenzo's funeral.

She'd thought his unusual lack of desire was due to grief and exhaustion. Now, another more awful reason invaded her mind...

Brooke groaned in despair.

Francesca's abrupt move back to Milan suddenly took on a more sinister meaning, as did Leo's whole-hearted approval of his sister-in-law's decision. He'd wanted the opportunity to be alone with the woman he still loved and wanted, away from the prying eyes of his family, and well away from *her*, his wife.

Francesca's tears that day might not have been grief, but guilt.

She was the type of female to feel guilty, Brooke thought bitterly, but not enough to say no to a determined man. If Leonardo declared his undying love for her, passionately insisting she give him what she'd once withheld, silly, wishy-washy Francesca would probably become as putty in his hands.

Now Brooke's eyes snapped up, and they were no longer quite so haunted-looking. They were angry. No, not just angry. Livid.

Giuseppe might be able to turn a blind eye to his son's adultery, but she could not! She would go and confront the pair of them. Right now! This very moment! Borrow Sophia's car and drive into Milan to Francesca's place.

She knew the way. Leo had often taken her into Milan to shop during previous visits, as well as to his brother's fancy apartment for those dinner parties. She herself had driven home on these occasions, forced to concentrate on the roads involved in a way you didn't when you were a passenger.

Leo liked to have a bottle of wine over dinner, and always gave her the keys at the end of such evenings. It was the only time he allowed her to drive when he was in the car, something which rankled Brooke but which she tolerated. As she'd tolerated Leo's edict shortly after their marriage that he didn't like *her* to drink much. He'd said it made her aggressive.

'Like your mother,' he'd added, when she'd been about to object.

That thought had stopped the automatic protest bubbling up in her throat, after which she'd curtailed her drinking, restricting herself to just one glass or two. Not once during the last five years of their relationship had she ever told Leo it was *his* turn not to drink that evening, that *she* wanted to relax over a bottle of wine for once.

'Silly, weak cow!' she sneered at herself in the bathroom mirror. 'No wonder he thinks he can get away with cheating on you.'

Well, he was in for a shock, wasn't he? In about an hour she would be arriving at Francesca's door, and there would be hell to pay!

If by some remote possibility Giuseppe was right, and Leo *wasn't* with Francesca, if it proved his car was parked safely in the Milan head office car park, and not where she suspected it would be, then she would simply turn round and drive home.

But some inner female instinct told her Leo wasn't going to be at the office, just as his mother knew. Women knew about such things, provided they opened their stupid eyes and saw the signs.

'Well, my eyes are well and truly open now, Leo,' Brooke seethed aloud. 'And God help you!'

With cold fury in her heart, Brooke set about brushing her hair and applying some lipstick before going downstairs in search of Leo's mother.

She found her in one of the large sitting rooms, ostensibly reading a magazine. But her grey head was bowed in a weary fashion, her normally proud shoulders slumped in an attitude of great sadness.

Brooke's heart squeezed tight. She liked her mother-in-law a lot. Sophia was a warm, generous-hearted woman who'd welcomed her into her home and her heart without question. How wretched she must be feeling, with one son dead and the other involved in a potentially disastrous affair.

Protecting Sophia from unnecessary distress became an instant priority with Brooke, her inner fury temporarily pushed to one side. She was still determined to go and find Leo, but whatever happened after that would be between them and them alone. Sophia was not to be told a thing.

Her mind made up, Brooke moved into the room. Sophia's head jerked up at the sound of footsteps on the tiled floor.

'Brooke!' she exclaimed. 'I...I thought you were sleeping.'

Brooke adopted what she hoped was a suitably wan expression. 'I tried. But I have this dreadful headache.'

'Oh, my dear. What a shame. Can I get you something? A tablet? A drink?'

'No. I'm afraid they won't help. It's a PMT thing. My period's due tomorrow.' Which it was, she realised.

Being on the pill, such things were very predictable. 'Happens every month. Sometimes, when I get this back home, I go for a walk or a drive. For some reason that unwinds me and the headache goes away. Would you mind if I borrowed your car, Sophia? I promise to be careful and not to speed.'

'Of course you can, dear. But where will you drive to?'

'Oh…just around.'

'Do you want me to go with you?'

'No, no. I prefer to be by myself. Would you mind the children for me if they wake up before I return?'

'Certainly.'

Five minutes later, Brooke was carefully negotiating the tight corners of the curving road which hugged the lake, only the prospect of leaving her children motherless stopping her from speeding.

She couldn't get to Milan fast enough. She wanted to see the evidence of Leo's betrayal for herself; wanted to see his car outside Francesca's apartment block; wanted to storm inside and find them together.

In her mind's eyes she saw herself tearing strips off Leo, shouting and screaming and doing all those hysterical things she hadn't done during her last five lily-livered years!

The drive took well over an hour, with traffic building the closer she got to Milan. Brooke got a bit lost before finally turning into the wide, tree-lined street which housed Francesca's apartment block.

Brooke had thought she was ready for the sight of Leo's car parked in one of the visitors' bays by the side of the building.

But she'd been wrong.

Her stomach cramped when her eyes landed on its distinctive make and colour, then heaved when the number-plate confirmed there was no mistake. She only just opened her own car door in time for her lunch to land in the gutter and not her lap. As it was, her dress became a little stained.

At last, she sank back against the leather seat, shaken and still shaking. All she could think of was that the man she loved… her husband…her Leo…was inside that building, inside Francesca's apartment, in her bedroom, in her bed.

No use pretending he wasn't. If his presence there was perfectly innocent, why lie about what he was doing today?

He'd probably been lying all week, Brooke accepted, nausea swirling again. He'd probably never been in the office at all. Or only minimally. That was why he'd left his mobile phone number with her, and not the office number.

Perversely, now that she had proof of his lies, her courage failed her. Suddenly she was afraid of what would happen if she did go inside and confront them both.

Because there would be no going back then: no pretending it was just a passing problem—or a passing passion; no turning that blind eye Giuseppe had perhaps wisely said was the only solution.

If she confronted them, her marriage would be over. Even if Leo didn't want that—and Brooke believed that Leo would not want to hurt or lose his children—then pride would come into it.

Her pride.

It was one thing to go on living with a man you knew didn't love you. Quite another to go on living with a man who knew you *knew* he didn't love you. That would be beyond the pale. Totally unendurable.

But she could drive away now, go back to the villa and pretend she knew nothing. Then, if Leo took them back to Australia this Friday—confirming he'd made the decision to give up Francesca for the sake of his family—they might be able to go on as before. Because that would mean he *did* love her, in a way.

Who knew? Maybe his being with Francesca today *was* just a sex thing, a hangover from the past, an old, unrequited passion which he hadn't been able to let go. Maybe he was doing exactly what his father said, getting the woman out of his system.

Much as it killed Brooke to think of Leo in the arms of another woman, it was better he take the creature to bed a few times then ask for a divorce.

The truth was she simply could not bear it if Leo divorced her. Brooke knew she would never love another man as she loved him. On top of that he was the father of her children. They adored him. Heavens, even her *mother* had grown to like him.

Better she swallow her pride and turn that blind eye. Better she ignore the pain, hide the overwhelming feelings of humiliation and pretend nothing had changed.

But oh, dear Lord, it was going to be hard...

Brooke swallowed, reached forward, and turned on the engine. Slowly, wretchedly, she turned the car and made her way back to Lake Como.

'My dear, you look *terrible*!' was Sophia's first remark on her return. 'And what's that on your dress?'

'I...I was sick,' Brooke mumbled, feeling wretched
and utterly exhausted. 'Must be a migraine, not PMT.'

'You poor thing. I know how terrible they are. I've
suffered from migraines for years. You simply must go
back to bed. And draw the curtains. I'll bring you up
some very good tablets the doctor prescribed for me.
They'll make you sleep, but that's for the best. Now,
don't you worry about the children. Giuseppe has taken
them out for a boat ride on the lake. Nina's gone with
them, so they'll be quite safe.'

Brooke was having a battle not to cry. 'You're very
kind,' she choked out.

'Not at all. Leonardo rang again. I didn't tell him
you were out driving. I said you had a headache and
were having a sleep. I hope I did the right thing.'

Brooke met the woman's worried eyes and wondered
why they were both protecting Leo.

For the sake of the children, she supposed.

'Yes, Sophia, you did the right thing,' she said in a
flat, dead voice.

'Good. Now, upstairs with you and into a nice re-
freshing shower. I'll put the tablets by your bed, along
with a drink and something light for you to eat. It's not
good to take these tablets on an empty stomach. And
don't worry about anything. If you're still asleep when
Leo comes home, I'll tell him not to disturb you.'

Now the tears came, and Sophia looked alarmed.
'Are you sure it's just a headache, Brooke? There's
nothing else wrong, is there?'

Brooke refused to add to the woman's worry. She'd

had enough on her plate lately. This was *her* problem and she would deal with it.

'I think I'm a bit homesick,' she said, not untruthfully.

Sophia nodded. 'It's time Leo took you home.'

Brooke just smiled sadly and turned to go upstairs. Her legs felt like lead, each step a mammoth effort. By the time she came out of the shower, two rather big white pills were sitting on the near bedside table, along with a glass of water. A small and very elegantly set out tray rested on the other table, with two tempting-looking sandwiches and a tall glass of iced milk.

Her mother-in-law's sweet thoughtfulness brought another rush of tears. Brooke knew Sophia would be devastated if she and Leo broke up. So would Giuseppe. Brooke could not do it to them, or to her children, or to herself. She loved Leo. She would always love him, no matter what. Life without him was unimaginable!

Brooke fell asleep with tears still wet on her cheeks. But they had long dried when she woke many hours later to the sounds of someone in the *en suite* bathroom, in the shower.

Her errant husband, it seemed, had finally deigned to come home.

CHAPTER THREE

ODDLY, Brooke's first reaction was fury, not distress.

The room was dark, she noted angrily. Leo must have turned the bedside lamp off when he came in.

She rolled over to check the luminous numbers on the bedside clock and saw it was twenty minutes past eleven. Not *too* late, so a wife wouldn't be suspicious. Certainly not one as stupidly doting and one-eyed as herself!

With a bitter resentment in her heart, she rolled back onto her side, facing the far wall, curling her body up in a foetal position, glad she was wearing one of her more modest nighties.

Leo had a thing for short, slinky black satin nightwear which barely covered her bottom. This particular nightie was much longer, reaching her knees. It was particularly low-cut up top, however, and had only the thinnest shoulder straps keeping it in place. Still, with her back to him, its length was the most important factor.

I'll pretend to be asleep, she vowed savagely as she lay there. That way I won't say anything I might regret in the morning.

Maybe if Leo hadn't stayed in the shower so darned long Brooke might have been able to keep to that vow. But fifteen minutes went by and the water was still running, evoking all sorts of darkly jealous thoughts.

He was trying to wash the smell of her off his body. He probably *reeked* of her, and that heavy, musky perfume she always wore.

By the time the taps were turned off, five minutes later, Brooke had rolled back over and was glaring in the direction of the bathroom, watching and waiting for him to come out.

She was still glowering at the door when it finally opened.

Leo emerged, obviously trying not to make a sound, turning off the bathroom light before carefully closing the door behind him.

But not before Brooke got a good long look at him, framed in the brightly lit doorway.

There was no doubting Leo was an impressive man naked. Brooke had never seen better.

He had it all. Broad shoulders. Deep chest. Flat stomach. Slim hips. Gorgeous olive skin. Not *too* much body hair. Strong arms and lovely muscular thighs...with more than adequate equipment in between.

Brooke had been overawed by him from the first time he'd stripped for her. She was still overawed by him. Even now, when she wanted to hate him.

Her heart began to pound as his darkened silhouette crossed the room, lifted the sheet and slid, still naked, into the bed. Not an unusual occurrence. Leo often slept in the nude.

But the cool, casual arrogance of the man infuriated her. When he rolled over and put his back to her, she wanted to kill him.

Brooke lay there, scowling up at the ceiling, thinking

of the cruellest most uncivilised way of putting him to death for his crimes against her and their marriage. The guillotine was too quick and too kind. The same applied to a firing squad. She wanted him to suffer as she was suffering, to *endure*...in agony.

Hanging, drawing and quartering would do just fine, she decided. Like in past times. But only after a few years' solitary confinement in one of those cold, old prisons, where his only companions would be cockroaches and rats!

Unfortunately, there was no real solace or satisfaction in such thinking, and Brooke's jealous fury was soon sidelined by an equally savage determination to know for sure just how great Leo's crimes against her were: how *far* things had progressed, how many *times* he'd been unfaithful to her that day.

The state of his body, she resolved with a wild recklessness, would be much more telling than the sight of his car in that car park this afternoon.

He flinched when her hand landed on the indent of his waist, then stiffened when it began to slide around further. Abruptly he rolled onto his back, his head twisting on the pillow to face her.

By this time the palm of Brooke's hand was resting provocatively on his stomach, and her heart was racing. With fear of what she'd find, she wondered? Or fear of what he'd do if she dared touch him down there?

'I thought you were asleep,' he said, his voice as cool as his skin.

'I was.' She could just make out his face. The moon was out and the curtains which covered the bedroom windows were light and filmy, letting in enough light to see by once your eyes had adjusted.

Leo was looking at her rather oddly, his eyes narrowed and wary.

'I tried to be quiet,' he said, a measure of defensiveness in his voice.

'Why?'

'Mamma told me you'd had a bad migraine all day. She said she'd given you some pills.'

'Yes. She did. She's very kind, your mum.'

'True.'

There was a moment's awkward silence when Leo said nothing further and Brooke's courage began to fail her. Her hand lay still on his stomach while her heart thudded away.

'You're very late, Leo...'

'Yes. I know. I'm sorry, but Lorenzo's left a damned awful mess behind him. I'm trying to have everything sorted out before we leave on Friday. I haven't finished yet, either. I wasn't as productive today as I would have liked to be. Too many interruptions. So I might have to work late tomorrow night as well.'

'I see,' Brooke said, and another awkward silence fell between them.

'It's not like you to have a migraine, Brooke,' Leo said at last. 'I wonder what brought it on?'

Thinking of you in love with Francesca all these years, she wanted to throw at him. *Thinking of you in bed with her all afternoon and half the night.*

Such thoughts renewed her bitter resolve to see the lie of the land, once and for all.

'I feel much better now,' she murmured, and slid her hand back and forth across his stomach.

He sucked in sharply.

'So I see,' he bit out.

When he made no move to stop her, Brooke's hand changed direction. A little shakily, it began to travel downwards, till it encountered then encircled her intended target.

Shock held her fingers still for a few moments. For never had Leo felt so limp, or less interested in her touch!

As Brooke had already found out this afternoon, it was one thing to *think* something, another to find hard evidence of its truth, even when that evidence wasn't hard, but soft. Crushingly, cruelly soft!

Waves of emotion swept through her. Dismay. Devastation. Despair! How could he betray her this way? Deceive her? *Destroy* her!

And how could Francesca? The bitch! And so soon after her husband's death!

Eventually, surprisingly, the wish to kill them both was sublimated by the mad desire to *make* Leo respond, to show him that she—his wife—knew him better than any other woman, knew what he liked, could give him pleasure unequalled elsewhere. Francesca couldn't possibly do for him what Brooke knew *she* could.

Finally, her frozen fingers began to move once more.

His groan sounded like a protest, but she stubbornly ignored it, using her acquired knowledge of his body to arouse him. After all, hadn't Leo tutored her personally in what he liked during the first few weeks of their relationship, spending long evenings and even longer nights in extending her sexual education, showing her at the same time that her previous lovers had been total ignoramuses?

All they'd wanted were quickies.

But his flesh was depressingly slow to respond, its lack-lustre performance very telling. Her normally responsive and very virile husband must have been making love all day to be like this!

Brooke refused to give up. He *would* respond, she vowed with an icy resolve, her heart hardening against any distracting or distressing emotions.

'This isn't like you, Leo,' she murmured, all the while caressing him intimately.

'I thought you were asleep,' he muttered through obviously gritted teeth. 'I've just had a very long, very cold shower.'

In truth, his skin *was* cold. But she didn't believe his lengthy shower had anything to do with consideration for her.

'Then maybe you need a little extra help,' she said, and, sliding down his body, boldly took the evidence of his recent betrayal between her lips.

This wasn't something Brooke ever did off her own bat. Only at Leo's behest. Even then, it wasn't something he asked for much nowadays. In fact she couldn't remember the last time. Probably last summer, here, in this very room. But in the past it had unfailingly aroused him, no matter how many times he'd already made love to her.

It aroused him now, his flesh swelling quickly. Brooke was merciless, her only aim to make him so excited that he would lose control. She wanted to seduce him so totally that he would forget everything else…and everyone else. Especially Francesca.

At the back of her mind Brooke knew she was acting out of sheer desperation, but she couldn't stop for the life of her. One part of her was almost horrified by what she was doing. Another part remained coldly detached, driving her on to do everything she could think of. And more. Her hands joined her lips in the fray, finding all sorts of erotic areas to torment and tantalise. She was more adventurous than she'd ever been before.

Dimly, she heard him moan, felt his own fingers splay shakily into her hair. When they tightened, she thought for one awful moment he was going to drag her away, make her stop.

But he didn't.

He muttered something in Italian at one stage, his voice low and shaking.

She stopped momentarily to glance up at him. His handsome face was etched clearly in the moonlight, his hooded eyes almost shut, his mouth grimacing.

'Do you want me to stop?' she purred.

When a violent shudder shook his head from side to side, she smiled an amazingly cool smile, dipped her head, and continued.

His breath began coming in raw, panting gasps. He was erect now, all right. More than he'd ever been, his flesh almost cruelly stretched. And straining.

A wave of dark triumph flooded Brooke, bringing its own brand of excitement and satisfaction. For at that moment Leo was hers, totally. He had no will of his own. No ability to think, let alone stop her.

Or so she'd thought.

Brooke was so caught up in her own dizzying sense of power that she didn't notice Leo's hands abandon her hair. When they slid under her arms and pulled her up off him, her cry of shock and frustration was very real.

Ignoring her protest, Leo pushed the satin nightie up to her waist, grasped her buttocks in an iron grip and lifted her till she was kneeling high above him. Before she knew it, his titanic erection was between her thighs and she was being forcibly drawn downwards onto it.

Her lips gasped wide at the swiftness of this turn-around, plus the stunning pleasure as her husband slid, hard and huge, into her. She hadn't realised till that moment how turned on she was.

So much for being removed from the experience!

So much for being the one in control!

Suddenly, all she wanted was to move, to feel him filling and refilling her. But he was holding her too tightly for the riding motion she craved. In desperation, she swayed back and forth, wriggling her hips and squeezing her insides to create some friction, to ease the craven need which was suddenly driving her wild.

'Be *still*!' Leo commanded, his thumbs and finger-tips digging into her flesh.

'But I don't *want* to be still,' she choked out.

'I can see that,' he growled, then smiled the wick-edest smile up at her. 'But I need a little time to compose myself before we continue. Still…maybe I can help *you* out in the meantime.'

His black eyes glittered in the moonlight as he reached up to brush her tangled hair back off her flushed face, pushing it right back off her shoulders before slowly sliding the thin straps off her shoulders, peeling the nightie downwards till her breasts were totally exposed.

Brooke knew, without looking at them, that they were cruelly swollen, and her nipples as hard as rocks. She had nice breasts. Big, without being too big. Breastfeeding had made them drop only a little, and her nipples were much larger than before.

'I should neglect you in the bedroom more often,' Leo muttered thickly, 'if this is the result.' Reaching up, he took both nipples between his thumbs and forefingers, and gave them both a sharp tug.

Shock—and something else—quivered down Brooke's spine. Leo had never done anything remotely like that to her nipples before. He was usually so gentle and tender with her breasts, using his mouth and tongue more than his hands.

When he did it again, Brooke wasn't sure if the sensation was pleasure, or pain. All she knew was it left her nipples with the most delicious burning feeling.

She stared downwards and saw they looked longer and harder than she'd ever seen them, brazenly standing out from her breasts, eager for more of the same. Leo took possession of them again, none too gently once more, rolling the still burning flesh between his fingers in a slow, twisting motion, bringing not a cry, but a moan. Of the most amazing pleasure.

'Do you want me to stop?' he murmured, echoing what she'd said to him earlier.

Excitement rendered her speechless. He laughed a

low, sexy laugh and then continued the delicious torment.

In the end she could not bear his eyes upon her, watching her gasp and squirm.

'Leo…please…'

'Please, what?' he drawled, obviously enjoying her breathless arousal. 'Stop? More? Tell me, *mi micetta*. I'll do anything you want. Though you're hardly a kitten tonight. More of a tiger. I think you'd have eaten me alive if I'd let you.'

'Leo, please,' she repeated huskily, her face flaming with both embarrassment and excitement.

'What is it you want me to do? Touch you down here…is that it? Like this?'

She stiffened, then groaned. No, no, not there, she agonised. And not like that.

Leo sometimes made her come first by touching her there. But never before when her body was displayed in such a vulnerable and exposed fashion, never with him watching her responses so blatantly.

Her stomach curled over at the thought.

But he kept touching her in exactly the right spot, and soon she just didn't care.

'Oh God,' she moaned, stiffening and squirming as she tried to hold on, not wanting the magic—or the madness—to end.

'Let yourself go,' Leo urged huskily. 'I want to watch you come. It's the ultimate turn-on for me, don't you know that, seeing you like this?'

Her mind spun at his words.

'Look at me, Brooke,' he commanded forcefully, and she did so, as though pulled by some irresistible magnet. And it was while her eyes were locked to his that her body did exactly what he wanted, splintering apart like fine crystal, her stomach sucking in as her back arched and her lips gasped wide.

Leo made some kind of animal sound, then pulled her down under him, surging into her like a man possessed. His pumping was so deep and wild that he came within seconds, well before her own violently electric spasms had faded away. She called out his name and he scooped her up off the bed, clasping her close, rocking them both to and fro while he shuddered into her. Rapturous tremors ricocheted down Brooke's spine as she clung to him and forgot everything but the moment.

It wasn't till the heat of their animal mating began to cool that sanity slowly returned.

So who seduced who in the end, darling? a coldly cynical voice challenged. Who totally lost control? And what, if anything, did you just prove?

Nothing, Brooke accepted wearily, except that you're still giving Leo the only thing he ever wanted from you besides his children. Your body. Your supposedly beautiful but very weak, traitorous body.

And you'll keep on giving it to him, won't you? You'll keep on humiliating yourself.

Some last pathetic vestige of pride compelled her to struggle against his breast-squashing hold, but she was too exhausted and he was too strong. Defeated, she laid her face back against his chest and began to weep, great racking sobs of despair.

'Hey, hey, what's this?' Leo unwrapped his arms to take her tearstained face in his hands, tipping it upwards.

She couldn't say a word, just looked up into his puzzled gaze with all the love and despair in her heart. *How could you do this to me?* she wanted to wail at him. *I gave you everything!*

I'm still *giving you everything.*

Her face crumpled anew at the thought.

'There, there,' he crooned, cradling her weeping face back against him and stroking her long hair down her back with tender hands. 'You got too excited, that's all. It happens that way sometimes, if you haven't had sex for a while.'

Gently, he lowered her back to her pillow, and even more gently withdrew.

'Hush now,' he murmured, stroking her hair back from her face. 'Stop crying and try to sleep, or you'll get another headache.' He kept stroking her hair and her head and gradually the tears stopped. Brooke just lay there in his arms, staring blankly up at the ceiling, trying not to feel a thing.

He continued stroking her hair and, speaking softly, gently, said, 'I know I haven't been much of a husband lately, but the past three weeks have been…difficult, to say the least. My brother's death has caused all sorts of problems, problems too complex and numerous to explain. Suffice to say I've sorted them out now.'

Brooke listened to this subtly worded confession without a shred of reassurance or forgiveness. How smooth he was, she realised. How clever. How *patronising*!

She closed her eyes against the temptation to look into his. For she knew she wouldn't see anything revealing there. Leo lied as well as he did everything else.

'I probably haven't told you this often enough,' he went on, bending to press his lips into her hair, 'but I *do* love you, Brooke…'

Brooke stopped breathing. How could words so longed for strike like daggers into her heart? And who exactly was Leo trying to convince with his far-too-late declaration?

Oh, Leo…Leo…

Brooke's soul wept, but her heart hardened. For she knew who her husband really loved. His own mother had said so. Francesca. The woman he'd once planned to marry.

But it was partly as Giuseppe had said. Leo would not want to lose his family, even for Francesca. So his wife was to be kept happy on the home front, keeping her suspicion-free.

Brooke was prepared to go to great lengths to save her marriage—hadn't she already shown that?—but she had to keep *some* self-respect. So she simply refused to hear the words, or recognise them, pride keeping her eyes tightly shut as she pretended to be sound asleep.

'Brooke?' Leo prompted softly after a few seconds. She remained steadfastly silent. Finally he sighed, then let her convincingly limp body slip out of his arms.

A bitter resentment burned through Brooke at the tender way he covered her with a sheet before rolling away from her onto his side. He really thought it was that easy, didn't he? Give the missus some great sex and a few sweet words and she'd be putty in his hands, never questioning what he did or where he went, leaving him scot-free to have it all. His wife, his children, *and* his mistress.

How he would manage to conduct such an affair from Sydney, Australia, Brooke had no idea. But she was convinced he would. Leo occasionally went overseas on business for a week or two. His father had agreed to his staying and living in Sydney five years ago provided he took on the role of troubleshooter for Parini International. In the early days she'd gone with him, but not now, not with two children in tow.

No doubt there would suddenly be more business trips abroad. Not necessarily to Milan—Leo was no fool!—but to New York, perhaps, or London, or Paris even. Places where the Parini family business had offices and luxury company apartments, places Francesca could fly to at a moment's notice and be bedded without anyone being any the wiser.

It wasn't as if Leo's comings and goings were ever reported in the tabloids or gossip columns. The Parini men had always kept a low profile publicity-wise. No doubt Leo would use the excuse of Lorenzo's death to increase such trips. And no doubt she would never be allowed to accompany him.

'A mother's place is with her children!'

Leo had made that firm statement when she'd brought up the subject of returning to work shortly after Claudia was born. She hadn't meant straight away. She'd meant when both children finally went to school. But Leo had been so adamant—and so shocked she could even *think* of doing such a thing—that she'd never brought the matter up again.

Brooke shook her head in despair over her past weaknesses, as well as her present. Leo would do what he wanted to do. And she wouldn't say a word. That was the truth of it, wasn't it?

But was this bravery or cowardice? There were so many things to be weighed up, so many people's happiness, not just her own. But how did you keep other people happy when you felt so miserable inside? How could you smile when you wanted to cry?

Tears blurred her eyes, but she blinked them away and turned over to face the far wall. She was damned if she was going to cry again. Tears never solved a thing, anyway.

Sleep didn't come for Brooke till just before the dawn, and by the time she woke again Leo had left for Milan, leaving a note on his pillow saying that after last night he would make sure not to be late home tonight.

She groaned at the wave of involuntary excitement which swept through her veins, her self-disgust as sharp as the shards of desire slicing through her. Her nipples went hard with the hot memory of what Leo had done to them last night. And what she'd done to him!

She was clutching the note in her hands, her cheeks burning and her stomach churning, when she remembered her period was due that day.

A sob of sheer relief escaped her lips. She simply couldn't have faced any more self-destructive behaviour.

Or many more days here, for that matter, she thought agitatedly as she swept on her dressing gown and hurried along to the children's rooms. She kept reassuring herself that in just over a day, they would be on their way home.

Once there, maybe she would be able to face Leo making love to her again without feeling so humiliated afterwards. At least Francesca would be thousands of miles away, and, perhaps more to the point, Leo could not have possibly made love to *her* that same day.

Brooke stopped momentarily outside the nursery door to take several deep, steadying breaths. Once composed, she plastered a smile on her face and reached for the doorknob.

Although called the nursery, it was really a large playroom, with wonderfully large windows, a sensibly tiled floor and enough toys to fill a kindergarten. When she went in, Claudia was busily setting up a tea party with three of her dolls. Alessandro was riding a large, life-like rocking horse over in a far corner. Nina, the Italian nanny, was sitting in a window-seat, perhaps admiring the lake.

It really looked very beautiful in the mornings, the water like glass.

Nina's head jerked round at the sound of the door opening. On seeing Brooke, she rose and smiled at her. 'Good morning, *signora*,' she said in English. She liked practising her English, and planned to visit Australia one day. 'You're looking much better today. You have colour in your cheeks.'

Brooke's cheeks coloured a little more at the remark. 'Yes,' she said briskly. 'My headache's gone. Thank you for looking after the children, Nina. I'll take over now.'

'I'll be down in the kitchen if you want me,' she said, still smiling her warm, placid smile. She was twenty, a plump but pretty girl, very sweet, and wonderful with children. Apparently she had several younger brothers and sisters, and helped her mother with them.

'Mummy, you're up very late,' Claudia said, without complaint but with some puzzlement. 'I missed you.'

'I missed you too, darling,' Brooke returned. 'Have you got a hug and a kiss for me?'

Claudia jumped up from the red plastic chair and came running on her solid little legs, hurling herself into Brooke's already outstretched arms.

Claudia was a hugger and a kisser. Alessandro was too, but after Leo's comment one day recently that too much of that would turn him into a Mummy's boy, Brooke had begun holding back a little with her son. Now, she saw Alessandro watching her with his sister, a jealous sulk on his beautiful mouth.

She put Claudia down and walked over towards Alessandro, who promptly jumped off the rocking horse and pretended to polish the saddle, his back to her.

'And do you have a kiss and hug for me too, my darling boy?' she said gently as she squatted down behind him.

He hesitated, then with a sob whirled and threw himself into her arms, his own arms wrapping tightly around her neck. 'What's wrong, Alessandro?' she asked, her heart catching with love and concern.

He pulled back, his big dark eyes glistening. 'I want to go home,' he cried. 'I miss Mister Puss.'

Brooke almost smiled, because she didn't think Mister Puss would be missing *him* too much. A ten-year-old Abyssinian, Mister Puss had been inherited from an elderly neighbour when the woman had had to go into a nursing home and couldn't look after the cat. Alessandro had just begun walking at the time, and had thought the cat was the best toy in the world, a moving, meowing stuffed toy, with a tail to pull, ears to poke and a big, soft furry stomach to sit or lie on.

'He's not a cushion!' Brooke had kept telling her son, but to no avail. Oddly, the cat had taken no steps to avoid his tormentor. He never hissed or scratched, or ran away when sat on, as he so easily could have. It was truly a mystery.

'I miss Mister Puss too,' she said. 'We'll be home soon.'

'Not soon enough!' he grumbled.

Brooke sighed. She couldn't agree more.

CHAPTER FOUR

AT LAST!

Brooke expelled a series of relieved sighs as she carried Claudia swiftly along the passageway towards the jumbo jet which would take them to Sydney. The connecting flight from Milan had been late, and her already strung-out nerves had begun to fray further. But they'd made it just in time.

The last thirty-six hours had been the most difficult of her life. She'd felt as if a bomb was ticking away inside her, about to explode. Outwardly she'd managed to kept her cool, saying all the right things to her in-laws, and acting as normal as possible with Leo.

But it had not been easy. A couple of times he'd given her an oddly puzzled look, as though he knew something was wrong with her but didn't know what.

Thinking of Leo had her glancing over her shoulder at him. He was quite a few paces behind her, walking along as cool and casual as you please, holding his laptop in one hand and Alessandro's hand in the other. The boy was striding out by his side, like the little man he liked to be when he was with his precious father. Nothing sissy for him like being carried.

Leo caught her eye and gave her one of his warm, intimate little smiles, the kind which once upon a time would have made her feel so wonderfully cared for and cared about.

Now, it set her teeth on edge.

She whipped her eyes forward before he could see the instant resentment flash into her eyes, and hurried on.

'Do you want *me* to carry Claudia?' he called after her, something in his voice telling her that he *had* picked up some negative vibe, if not in her eyes then in her manner.

'No, thank you,' she replied crisply without turning round. 'I'm fine.'

As fine as you can be when you're living a lie, she thought bitterly. When the love you once felt for your husband is gradually changing to contempt. When your heart is bleeding to death and your marriage is nothing but a sham!

Unfortunately, Brooke *had* to look back at Leo once she'd stepped on the plane and the flight attendant had put out her hand for her boarding pass. She didn't have it. Leo was carrying all four passes.

'My husband has them,' she tautly informed the very pretty girl, nodding towards Leo as she stepped to one side and turned around.

It was another eye-opening education, watching the flight attendant with Leo. Brooke had always known women found him overwhelmingly attractive. Waitresses rushed to do his bidding without delay. Shop girls simpered all over him. Women on the street would stare openly as he walked by.

This had never bothered her before, because she'd been secure in her marriage and had trusted her husband implicitly. Besides, Leo had never seemed to notice the stares, or the fawning attention. Whenever they were together he'd seemed to have eyes only for her. He'd never done anything to make her jealous, so she'd never *been* jealous.

Not so any more. A black jealousy now festered within her soul, making her fume at the way the flight attendant's face lit up when she saw Leo, the way the woman's green cat-like eyes gleamed in that very female yet predatory way as they raked over him.

Of course Leo was looking superb—and sexy as hell—in a charcoal-grey suit and a black crew-necked top. Any woman would have fancied him.

But did that mean she had to smile at him in that sickening way in front of *her*, his wife? Didn't she have any sense of diplomacy, or decency?

No, Brooke realised ruefully. Where men like Leo were concerned, it was open season these days. Especially if they didn't love their wives…

Brooke suddenly felt sick. Maybe Francesca would prove the least of her problems in the long run. Maybe she was trying to save a marriage and keep a husband who could *not* be kept, no matter what humiliations she endured or how many blind eyes she turned.

'Your seats are on the flight deck, sir,' the attendant purred. 'Up those stairs and to the left. The third row from the front, the two seats on each side of the aisle.'

'Thank you,' Leo returned with his usual polite, pleasant manner. Yet to Brooke his returning smile seemed slightly flirtatious this time, his eyes lingering far too long on the female's moist mouth. Was her imagination playing tricks on her, or was she suddenly seeing the real Leo behind the façade?

When he glanced over at Brooke she hoped she didn't look as despairing as she felt.

A brief frown flittered across his face before he bent down to talk to his son. 'You go up first, Alessandro. And here…you can carry my laptop, if you promise to be very careful with it. Did you hear what the young lady said just now? Our seats are three rows from the front. You can count to three, can't you?'

'I can count to ten!' Alessandro answered, pride in his voice.

'Of course you can. You're a clever boy. In that case, three won't be any problem at all. When you get to three, sit down in one of the window seats and put the laptop on the one next to you. We'll all be with you shortly.'

Alessandro scampered off up the steps to do his daddy's bidding and Leo turned to Brooke. 'Now,' he said firmly, and took his sleepy daughter out of his wife's arms. 'I'll take missie. She's much too big for you to carry up those steps. Especially in that get-up,' he added, with a wry glance down at her outfit.

Brooke gave no reply to this, just whirled round and began mounting the admittedly steep and quite narrow steps.

Immediately she saw what Leo meant. The long, narrow skirt she was wearing restricted movement, despite the split in the back seam, pulling tight around her bottom each time she lifted her foot up to the next step.

'Nice view,' Leo drawled from right behind her.

The sexually charged remark flustered Brooke. For one thing, it wasn't like Leo to make such comments. What flustered her most, however, was her own instant intense awareness of her bottom, and the way it was moving, barely inches from his face.

Brooke wished with all her heart that she was wearing something much less revealing, and much, much looser.

It *had* crossed her mind that morning not to get as dolled up as she usually did when travelling with Leo. But she could hardly stop dressing the way she usually dressed, not if she wanted to pretend nothing was wrong.

Leo always looked a million dollars when in public. Everyone would have thought it very strange if *she'd* shown up today garbed in tracksuit pants and sweatshirt.

So she'd put on the designer suede suit Leo had bought for her the previous year in a boutique in Milan, teamed it with a cream cashmere top and slipped on high heels which matched the colour of the suit—a deep camel shade.

Leaving her hair down would have been impractical, so she'd put it up, made up her face, added gold jewellery, then presented herself downstairs in her usual well-groomed state, if not her usual composed inner self.

She'd imagined—mistakenly—that getting on this plane would solve some of her problems, that she would calm down once Milan—and Francesca—were far behind them. But suddenly Brooke realised that wasn't going to be the case, because she'd brought the problem with her.

Leo was the problem. Leo, who could still make her do things and feel things, almost against her will. Leo, whom she still loved, even while she hated him. Leo, who at that very moment was behind her, coveting her sexually despite being in love with another woman.

What a wicked, ruthless man she was married to!

Face flaming, she reached the top of the stairs, where another attractive female waited in attendance, ready to take jackets whilst pointing out the many added advantages of flying business class on the flight deck. The on-tap galley down at the back. The toilets front and back. The personal televisions attached to each seat.

Brooke handed the woman her jacket, which had been draped over her arm, then proceeded along the aisle to where Alessandro was sitting in his seat, already strapped in. When she went to pick up the laptop and sit next to him, her son gave her a rather disdainful look.

'You can't sit there, Mummy. That's Daddy's seat. Daddy always sits next to me on planes,' he told her.

This was true. Alessandro was not an easy child to contain and control, especially during long flights. He was given to boredom when awake, and became very grizzling and difficult to handle when tired. He didn't drop off to sleep as easily as Claudia, and didn't *need* as much sleep as his younger sister.

They'd found that he was much better behaved if Leo sat next to him.

Leo, unlike some Italian fathers, was not over-indulgent. He gave Alessandro plenty of love and attention, but still expected him to be well behaved when with him, especially in public. He didn't discipline him physically. Just one dark, displeased glare from his father's eyes was enough to curtail the child, and make him think twice about his antics.

Brooke understood just how Alessandro felt when his father scowled at him like that. Leo had a very powerful personality, and a very powerful gaze. When he turned those half-hooded deeply set black eyes on you, he could make you do exactly what he wanted. Either because you wanted to, or because you were afraid *not* to.

When she'd first met Leo, they'd seduced her in seconds, those eyes. She'd been in his bed that very first night.

Brooke suddenly had the ghastly feeling Leo would want to sit next to her on the flight home.

And she simply could not bear the prospect.

Ignoring her son's protest, she swept up Leo's laptop and practically threw it onto the seat opposite. A swift glance down the back of plane showed the flight attendant holding a now wide awake Claudia whilst Leo shrugged smoothly out of his suit jacket. The woman was smiling at him in a similar flirtatious manner to the one downstairs.

Typical! Brooke thought savagely, and plonked herself down next to Alessandro.

'Daddy's sitting next to Claudia this time,' she informed her instantly sulking son. 'And don't you make a fuss,' she warned darkly, 'or you'll be sorry!'

Alessandro stared at this rather frightening new mother with a measure of shock in his big dark eyes.

'What's this?' Leo said when he came alongside, Claudia in his arms. 'Are you sure that's where you want to sit, Brooke?' he asked, and she glared up at him.

'I thought it was time Claudia had a turn sitting next to you,' she said rather sharply.

'Daddy!' Claudia's large velvety eyes lit up in a fashion which Brooke found very irksome. *Your father is just a man, not some god*, she wanted to snap at their daughter.

Leo hesitated, frowning down at Brooke.

She wrenched her eyes away from that penetrating gaze and stared out through the window onto the tarmac below. Not that she could see much except lights winking. It was pitch-black outside.

'Till you go to sleep, perhaps,' Leo conceded. 'Then I think we might change the arrangements. I wish to sit with your mother at some time.'

Brooke's stomach clenched down hard. She knew it. She just *knew* it!

'What about me?' Alessandro wailed.

'A big boy like you doesn't need me to babysit him any longer,' Leo said as he popped the laptop into the overhead luggage rack then bent over to settle Claudia in the window seat. 'Meanwhile, you can look after your mother for me,' he threw over his shoulder at Alessandro. 'She seems a little stressed out today. You know how she hates flying.'

Brooke tried not to stare at the way Leo's trousers pulled tight over his buttocks as he leant over Claudia's seat. But it was a bit hard not to look when she was only a couple of feet away, with her eyes level.

Leo had a great behind. Hell, he had a great everything. That was part of her problem. If only he'd grown flabby and bald and unattractive. If only she didn't still fancy him so darned much!

She was staring at his derrière with ill-concealed lust when Leo's head twisted further around to look right at her. Her eyes jerked up to his, but it was too late, and the hint of a smug little smile began to tug at the corners of his mouth.

Brooke battled to keep from blushing but she failed miserably. Not for the first time during the past couple of days, she was grateful she had her period. For Lord knew what Leo might have persuaded her to do during this flight if she hadn't been indisposed. It seemed finding out that her husband was a liar and an adulterer did not automatically turn her off him in a sexual sense.

Perversely, Brooke was finding she wanted Leo now more than ever before. She wondered if this was Mother Nature's way of making sure the family unit survived. Or was it just life having the last laugh on her for loving a man so blindly, and so obsessively?

'I'll look after Mummy for you, Daddy,' Alessandro said, all puffed up with pride at being asked to do such a grown-up job. 'I can set up her TV for her too. Mummy's not very good at doing things like that. She gets mad with the video at home sometimes, and says naughty words.'

'Really?' Leo said as he sat down, bringing his face almost down to her level. 'I can't imagine that,' he murmured across the aisle, his amused gaze dancing all over her heated face. 'Not *your* mummy. Not your perfect, ladylike mummy.'

'She does too, Daddy,' Alessandro insisted, even

while Brooke's face whipped round to glower at her big-mouthed son.

The sudden movement of the plane backing out of its parking bay, and the captain announcing they would soon be taking off, brought a welcome end to *that* little episode. And none too soon, in Brooke's opinion. She'd been about to combust!

The distraction of take-off and the serving of dinner and drinks soon afterwards was also very welcome. Both parents were fully occupied with their charges, making sure they didn't spill their drinks all over their laps.

After the meal, there were trips to the toilet, shoes to be removed, socks put on, television programmes to be selected, seats to be tipped back. The ever-attentive female flight attendant brought pillows and blankets for the children, fussing over them as if they were *her* children. No doubt she would have liked them to be, Brooke thought sourly as the woman flashed Leo another dazzling smile.

Finally, it was time for the lights to be dimmed in the cabin. Almost immediately Claudia fell fast asleep, and lo and behold so did Alessandro, the little traitor. Brooke could not believe it!

When Leo leant over the aisle towards her, she stiffened in her seat.

'Best we move Claudia over to your seat,' he whispered. 'She won't stir for anything.'

'Why don't we just leave them be, Leo?' she suggested in desperation.

'No,' he said firmly. 'I want to talk to you. And *not* leaning over an aisle all the time.'

Knowing there would be no rest till she agreed, Brooke sighed and stood up, moving out of the way while Leo scooped up an unconscious Claudia and settled her in the seat next to her brother.

Brooke's heart caught as she watched her husband's tenderness with his little daughter. The way he arranged her pillows and tucked her in, the way he kissed her cheek, then Alessandro's.

She knew then that nothing would make Leo ask her for a divorce. He would stay married to her whether he loved her or not.

He straightened and smiled at her. 'Peace at last,' he said with a sigh. 'And privacy. You take the window seat, my sweet. I rather like the thought of having you imprisoned against a wall, with no escape but to climb over my lap.'

Brooke gritted her teeth when he took her by the elbow and ushered her quite forcefully into the window seat.

'Can I help you with that?' he said, leaning over to do up her seat-belt. She sat stiffly in her seat while he did so, trying not to thrill at his nearness, or the brush of his arms across her instantly taut breasts. Afterwards his head lifted, and their mouths were only inches away. She gulped at the look in his eyes, then gasped when he closed the distance between their lips.

It was a long, slow, tongue-in-her-mouth kiss which set her head spinning and her heart racing.

'Leo, stop it,' she protested breathlessly when his mouth lifted momentarily for a breather.

'Stop what?'

'Stop embarrassing me. People might see us.'

'Nearly everyone's asleep,' he murmured as he slid a hand around her neck and stared deep into her eyes. 'Either that or watching television. But I'm not sure I care, anyway. You look so beautiful and sexy today that you've been driving me insane. To be honest, you've been driving me insane since the other night. I can't stop thinking about what you did to me, especially with this lovely mouth of yours...'

His thumb-pad traced over her mouth and her lips fell apart once more, still wet and tingling from his kisses.

'You have such beautiful lips,' he murmured. 'You have no idea how they feel, or how glorious it is to watch your wife do that, to know she *wants* to do it. You've never done that before without my asking you to. God, I can't wait for you to do it again.' He began to insert his thumb into her mouth, and she almost, *almost* sucked it.

'Leo, for pity's sake,' she gasped, slapping his hand away. 'I...I can't. Not here. I *can't*!'

He looked surprised, as though it had never occurred to him that she could, or would. But oh, dear Lord, she might have, if he'd insisted. She was dizzy with the thought of it, drugged by the darkness of her own desires.

Confusion and dismay crashed together to create a very real distress, tears pricking at her eyes. How could she keep wanting him like this when she knew it was only sex with him?

'No, of course you can't,' he murmured, frowning at her distraught face. 'I'm sorry if I've upset you. I didn't mean to. I would never ask you to do anything you didn't want to do. Hell, Brooke, don't *cry*! I misinterpreted the way you were looking at me earlier. I thought... Damn it all, what does it matter what I thought now? Clearly I was wrong.'

He reached out and pulled her into his arms. 'Come here... Hush... Don't cry now... You're tired, that's all... Travelling with the children is always stressful... But we'll be home soon and then we can get back to our normal life. Okay?' He put her away from him and stared searchingly into her tear-washed eyes. 'Forgive me?'

She merely blinked and said nothing.

He sighed. 'You must understand how incredible you were the other night. I wouldn't be a normal man if I didn't want you to do it again. But I honestly didn't mean here. I would never do anything to hurt you or humiliate you. Never!'

At this, Brooke's eyes welled up again, and Leo pulled her back into his arms, apologising profusely.

Brooke *wanted* to forgive and forget—everything! But forgiveness simply would not come. She could feel something else building up inside herself, something cold and alien, something dark and dangerous, something strong and violent.

It was there now, deep inside, muttering away.

You've compromised enough already in this marriage, it growled. Time to make a stand. Time to show this unfaithful lying bastard he can't get away with what he's done. Time to take him on!

Brooke shuddered at where such actions would lead. Straight to the divorce court. Do not pass 'Go'! Do not collect two hundred!

Yet it had its appeal all right, she thought, even as she lay, weeping quietly, in his arms. She would just love to see the look on his face when he found out she knew all about Francesca, then his panic when he realised he might lose custody of his children. Suddenly she understood why people said revenge was sweet.

But it was also self-destructive.

Her emotions were tearing her this way and that. Poor Hamlet really had her sympathy.

To be or not to be, that was the question!

She really needed to talk to someone, someone who would see things more clearly and who wasn't going to have emotion cloud the issues. Someone who might be able to tell her what to do for the best.

Not her mother. Oh, dear heaven, no. She needed someone who wasn't warped and twisted, who would appreciate what she was trying to do: not only save her marriage, but protect her children's happiness.

It would have to be someone else.

But who?

CHAPTER FIVE

LEO had booked a car to be waiting for them at Mascot airport, thank heavens. The last thing she could have coped with at that moment was standing in a taxi queue for ages.

Brooke wondered if she looked as bad as she felt as she traipsed through Customs, a floppy Claudia in her arms. An equally sleepy Alessandro was draped over Leo's shoulder just ahead of them. Their luggage was in a trolley, which Leo was pushing somewhat wearily with his spare hand.

He always said that was the worst thing about living in Australia—the distance they had to travel to see his family, or for him to go overseas on business. But he'd also said he would never want to bring up his children anywhere else. He liked the easy-going lifestyle, the weather, the space, and the relatively low crime rate.

The flight had felt interminable this time to Brooke, despite both children sleeping for most of it. Brooke had slept too, but not for nearly as long as she'd pretended. They'd touched down for a short stop at Bangkok, during which Brooke hadn't even bothered to leave the plane. Leo had, saying he needed to stretch his legs. He'd taken the children with him.

Brooke had been glad to see him go, experiencing an immediate easing of tension the moment he was out of sight.

Was that how it was going to be from now on? she worried as she came through the exit gate. Holding onto herself whenever he was around, then feeling relative relief once he'd gone out through the front door? And all the while having to endure this *thing*, this maelstrom of emotion whirling deep within her, turning tighter and tighter.

Eventually something—or someone—was sure to snap.

The driver from the car company was waiting for them just outside the exit gate, holding a card with their name printed on it. Leo introduced himself and handed the man the trolley with the luggage.

'This way,' the chauffeur said, and set off with the trolley.

'Is the car far away?' Leo asked after they'd followed him some distance through the long arrivals terminal.

'Not too far.' He led them towards a glass-doored exit through which Brooke could see a long, makeshift walkway with high boarded sides.

'I hope not,' Leo returned. 'My family's very tired, poor darlings,' he added, throwing Brooke a soft smile.

Brooke hated herself for deliberately turning her face away from him. But she simply could not stand the loving warmth in his eyes. Was it her imagination again, or was Leo being extra considerate to her? Extra affectionate?

He'd always been a caring husband, when he'd thought to be. But he'd been *so* attentive during the flight it had been almost sickening. Nothing had been too much trouble. If he'd asked her once if she was all right, he'd asked her a thousand times!

Guilt, she decided with a stab of resentment. For what else could it be? Why should he suddenly act differently with her?

'Everything's a bit of a mess here at Mascot at the moment,' the chauffeur explained as they trailed after him through the automatic doors. 'What with all the extensions for the Olympics. Hopefully everything will be back to normal soon. The car's just down here, to the right.'

The air was cool and crisp outside the terminal, with not a cloud in the sky. But the sun was sure to come out later, warming Sydney to a very pleasant autumn temperature.

The car was parked just around the corner, as the driver had said, a white stretch limousine with plush grey upholstery and tinted windows. The luxury of the car surprised Brooke. Leo was certainly pulling out all the stops, she thought sourly.

Brooke climbed into the car first, and deliberately buckled Claudia in on the back seat next to her, leaving Leo to sit next to Alessandro on the seat opposite.

But the ploy backfired when Leo chose the seat facing her, which was more awkward than having him sit next to her. He kept looking straight into her eyes, and frowning his obvious bewilderment at her manner.

Brooke sighed inwardly and turned her face towards the tinted window. It was a relief to be home, she conceded. But being home wasn't going to make everything right overnight.

Claudia stirred beside her.

'Mummy?' she said in slightly worried little-girl voice.

'Yes, sweetie?'

'I want to do a wee-wee.'

'Me too,' Alessandro piped up, before throwing an anxious look up at his father.

Brooke had to smile. At least her children didn't act differently.

'Okay,' Leo said with gritted teeth. 'Everyone out again.'

Whilst waiting for Claudia in the restroom, Brooke tidied her hair and freshened up her face, her reflection in the large mirror showing not a trace of the emotional distress she was still feeling. She didn't even look tired any more.

Brooke was amazed. It just showed the miracles good make-up could perform, though her mother would have said it was her age.

'You can bounce back in your twenties,' she would often moan. 'You can even look good after staying up all night. But wait till you pass forty. You look exactly how you feel in the mornings, or worse. Like you've been dragged through the mill. You mark my words.'

Brooke rarely marked her mother's words. Pity, as it turned out. She'd warned her about Leo but she simply hadn't listened.

Leo and Alessandro were already in the car and buckled up by the time she returned with Claudia.

'You look a hundred per cent better,' her husband said as she climbed in after her daughter. 'I was beginning to get worried about you.'

His comments irked her, as did his ongoing solicitous attitude. Her eyes were cold as they clashed with his. 'We women are easily fixed up,' she bit out before she could stop herself. 'But some repair jobs are only skin-deep, Leo. You'd be wise to remember that.'

Brooke gained no satisfaction from the stunned expression on her husband's face, or his obvious inability to respond to what must seem to him a very strange remark.

Was this the beginning? she thought despairingly. Of the unravelling? Of the end?

Dropping her eyes away from Leo's now frowning face, she attended to Claudia's seat-belt, next to her, then managed to further avoid his penetrating gaze for a while by fiddling with her own seat-belt.

Meanwhile, the car slid away from the kerb, and Alessandro started pestering his father about the cat.

'Can we go past Nanna's place to pick Mister Puss up on the way home, Daddy?'

'Not this morning, Alessandro. Your nanna lives way over town at Turrumurra, nearly an hour's drive from our place. Your mother can take you over there tomorrow to get him while I'm at work.'

Brooke's eyes whipped up to stare at her husband. 'You're going to work tomorrow?' she asked, her suspicions immediately aroused. 'On a *Sunday*?'

Leo *never* worked on a Sunday. A Saturday, maybe, but never Sunday. Sunday was family day. He always spent it with them. Often he took them out somewhere. The beach. The zoo. A picnic. Adventureland. The movies. Why was he rushing to work *this* Sunday? What was so important? Did he need the privacy of his office to telephone his beloved Francesca, to talk sweet nothings in her ear, plan their next romantic rendezvous perhaps?

His expression was weary, she thought. '*Today's* Sunday, Brooke. Tomorrow's Monday. We lost a day travelling back.'

'Oh. Oh, yes. I forgot. Stupid me.' Which she was. Stupid, stupid, stupid! Though not as stupid as he thought she was. 'If that's the case,' she said tautly, 'then my mother will be at work tomorrow *too*.'

Leo shrugged. 'Does it matter? You have keys to her place. You can still pick up the cat.'

'Does it occur to you I might like to *see* my mother?' Brooke said waspishly. 'That I might have missed her?'

Leo looked taken aback. 'I think perhaps you *are* still tired. It's not like you to be so snappy. I was just saying it as it is, Brooke. Besides, I wouldn't say you're ever *that* anxious to visit your mother.'

Brooke's chin shot up defiantly. 'My mother and I are a lot closer than you think.' And a lot more *like* each other than you think, buster, came that other dark, hard voice.

It certainly set Brooke thinking. Maybe she'd been wrong to dismiss the idea of confiding in her mother. She was beginning to think her mother's advice might be just what she needed to hear. Because she could not go on like this. Not for long, anyway.

'I'll drive over today,' she said curtly. 'While the children are having their afternoon sleep.'

'But I want to go and visit Nanna too, Mummy,' Alessandro piped up.

'Me too,' Claudia joined in.

'Not today,' Brooke said sharply. 'Today you can

stay at home and your father can mind you. I need to talk to my mother about something. Alone.'

'About what?' Leo asked, his eyes puzzled.

'Mother and daughter things,' Brooke retorted. '*Women* things. I'm sure you wouldn't be interested.'

'Are you referring to that bad headache you had recently? My mother said you told her it might be a PMT problem. I never knew you suffered from PMT, Brooke. You never mentioned it before.'

'What's PMT?' Alessandro asked.

'Poor mothers travelling,' Brooke whipped back as quick as a flash.

Leo laughed and leant forward slightly, bringing his face disturbingly close to hers. 'That was quick,' he murmured, his dark eyes dancing with dry amusement. 'You know, you're much cleverer than you let on sometimes, aren't you?'

Brooke's hands clenched tightly in her lap as she resisted the urge to slap him right across his smugly handsome face.

'You mean considering I'm a dumb blonde?'

He leant back abruptly, his smile fading, his mouth thinning. Leo was an intelligent man, but he was used to his wife not causing any waves in his life.

'You really *are* in a touchy mood. I'll try not to take offence. I'll blame it on the flight and the time of the month. But I sincerely hope you're in a better frame of mind come Wednesday.'

'Wednesday? What's on Wednesday?'

His eyebrows arched. 'It's our anniversary.'

'Oh. Oh, yes. I'd forgotten for a moment.'

His eyebrows arched further.

'What's a nannaversary?' Alessandro asked. 'Is it something to do with Nanna?'

'No, son,' Leo said, his eyes remaining on Brooke. 'It's like a birthday. On Wednesday, it's five years to the day since I married your mother.'

'Are we going to have a big party like when I turned four?'

'No. You don't have a big party till you've been married at least twenty-five years.'

Brooke almost laughed. At the rate they were going, they'd be lucky to make it to six!

'Till then,' Leo continued, 'each year, husbands take their wives out somewhere special for a private party. Just the two of them. This year I have a special treat in mind for your mother. I hope she has something special in mind for me too.'

Brooke stared at him, colour zooming into her cheeks as various images filled her mind.

'Do you get presents?' Claudia asked her father eagerly.

'Of course,' Leo replied, smiling at his daughter.

'Will you get Daddy a present, Mummy?' Claudia asked her mother with bright, excited eyes. Claudia was a born shopper. Present-buying ranked right up there with pretty clothes and dolls.

'We'll see, darling,' she said, glad to have an excuse to look away from Leo's suddenly smouldering gaze.

'Your mother doesn't have to buy me a present this year, Claudia,' Leo said silkily. 'I'll settle for something money can't buy.'

'What's that, Daddy?' Alessandro asked. 'Nonno in Italy says there's nothing money can't buy.'

'Oh, he does, does he? Well, Nonno has been known to be wrong. I'm talking about love, son. You can't buy love.'

No, Brooke thought despairingly. You can't. Otherwise she'd sell or pawn everything she owned to buy her husband's love.

But Leo wasn't talking about love. He was talking about sex. The sort of hot, wild sex she'd given him the other night. Regardless of what he felt for Francesca, he still fancied *her* in bed, maybe now more than ever. She'd shown him a new side to herself the other night, and he was eager to see that side again.

Brooke hadn't really achieved anything by her performance the other night. All she'd done was make Leo think she loved him more than ever.

Perverse as it was, that seemed to be the case. Even worse, she was already looking forward to Wednesday night. How sick could she get?

But it explained why she was being so snakey. Because she despised herself for still loving him.

'That's true, Leo,' she said, a touch bitterly. 'But an actual present might last longer. Ah, here we are. That was a short trip. It's an advantage living so close to the airport, isn't it? Still, there's not much traffic at this time in the morning. Come along, children, undo your seat-belts and let's go see if your rooms are still there.'

Brooke steered her children out onto the pavement and in through the front gate, along the old stone path towards the front steps, doing a quick survey of the front yard as she hurried by. Fortunately, the lawn and garden didn't look too bad for having been neglected for over three weeks. Grass didn't grow much in the autumn, and their garden consisted mostly of flowering shrubs.

She had her house keys ready in her hand by the time she'd mounted the front steps and swiftly inserted the right key in the door, leaving Leo behind to pay the driver and carry in the luggage. As soon as she pushed open the door, the children dashed inside ahead of her and ran up the hallway. Brooke followed more slowly, glancing in the living rooms as she went.

Home at last. *Her* home.

The house wasn't anything flash to look at from the street, just a simple federation-style cottage with a red roof, dark brick and stained glass windows.

Leo had bought the place because it was only a five-minute drive from his warehouse and office complex at Botany, with the added bonus of being close to the airport. He hadn't consulted Brooke in the purchase, and she had the feeling she'd passed some sort of test when she'd loved it on sight, and hadn't complained it wasn't grand enough.

In truth, she thought it was a lovely home, with a warm, cosy feeling to the rooms plus the most beautiful view over Botany Bay from the glassed-in front porch. She would have been happy living in it exactly as it was, but Leo had immediately brought in the renovators.

Initially, there had only been three bedrooms and one bathroom, a largish kitchen, an L-shaped lounge-dining room, a small sunroom, and a separate laundry shed out at the back. All these rooms had been retained in essence, but the back wall had been knocked out and the house extended to include a huge rumpus room, plus a guestroom with a second bathroom attached. The sunroom had become a large internal laundry, and the old laundry a garden shed. The only other change had been to the master bedroom, which was fortunately large enough to have had an elegant *en suite* bathroom included in one corner without sacrificing too much space.

Brooke had had a lot of fun decorating the house from top to toe. Initially, she'd been afraid Leo would insist on filling the house with Italian furniture and art-work, the kind he imported. She'd had visions of the cream-painted rooms filled to overflowing with the sort of dark, heavy, ornate pieces which really needed villa-style rooms in which to look good.

But thankfully Leo hadn't wanted to recreate a smaller version of his family villa out here. He seemed only too happy to have an Australian-style home, and had given Brooke a totally free hand in the decorating, plus a very generous budget. She could have spent a small fortune on furniture and furnishings from the most expensive shops in Sydney, but she had always hated that kind of indulgence, and instead had bought simple but solid pieces from major chainstores. She'd haunted their half-yearly sales and secured some fan-tastic bargains.

It always gave her pleasure to walk through the house and see what she'd achieved with a relatively small amount of money. Okay, so she didn't have an-tiques in every corner, or old masters hanging on the walls. But Brooke knew her home was beautiful to look at and comfortable to live in, with a simple style and understated elegance.

As for art… The pictures on the walls had been chosen because they were pleasing to the eye and suited the rooms in question, both in colour and content. Many a time her well-heeled dinner guests had commented on and complimented them, and, whilst the frames were high quality, not one picture was an original.

I would hate to lose my home, Brooke thought as she wandered down the hallway.

And I might, she realised with a sudden pang of dismay, if I don't get a grip on myself. I'm acting like a fool. An irrational, emotional, jealous fool.

But she couldn't seem to get a grip. She was on a roller-coaster ride to hell!

'Mummy, my room's still here,' Claudia trilled, tugging at her skirt. 'And so are all my dollies.'

'Of course your room's still here, silly,' Alessandro said, though he'd just come out of his own room looking as pleased as Punch. 'Mummy was just joking,' he said, and smiled the most incredible smile up at Brooke. So sweet and so open and so innocent.

'Yes, Mummy was just joking, darling,' she said, sweeping her son up into her arms and smothering his dear little face with kisses.

'I can see home's done the trick,' Leo said from the other end of the hallway. He dropped the suitcases he was carrying and walked down towards where the three of them were standing clustered together. 'I hope you've left some of Mummy's kisses for Daddy,' he said to Alessandro.

'No!' Alessandro pouted, and wrapped his arms tightly around Brooke's neck. 'I've taken them all.'

'I have enough kisses for everyone,' Brooke said, thinking of Claudia listening with jealous little ears.

'That's good to hear,' Leo whispered.

Brooke stiffened inside, dark, angry thoughts resurfacing with a vengeance.

So it was back to sex again, was it? Was that all he ever thought about? Or was his revitalised passion for her simply because the woman he *really* wanted was no longer available?

'Could I hope for some decent coffee as well?' he added.

Brooke put Alessandro down before straightening to face her husband. 'You can hope,' she muttered under her breath, 'but you might not get.'

Their eyes clashed. Leo's hardening gaze would have frightened her on any other day. But not *that* day.

'Go wash your face and hands, children,' Brooke instructed them coolly, while Leo glowered at her. 'Then come sit up at the table for some breakfast.'

They raced off to the bathroom, leaving husband and wife momentarily alone.

'What in God's name has got into you?' Leo growled.

'I don't know what you mean,' she said with false sweetness, and swanned off into the kitchen.

Leo was hot on her heels. 'You know *exactly* what I mean,' he muttered from right behind her. 'Don't play dumb with me, Brooke.'

She whirled, her expression scornful. 'Why not? You've always liked it before.'

His face showed true shock.

She smiled. She actually smiled.

She was behaving like a right bitch. But she couldn't seem to help herself.

When she went to walk over to the fridge he grabbed both her arms and spun her round to face him, his fingers digging with bruising strength into her flesh.

She stared down at his hands, then up into his furious eyes, her own like ice. 'Take…your…hands…off…me,' she said, punctuating each word.

He released her immediately, his face anguished as his hands lifted to rake through his hair. Brooke had never seen him look so distressed, and this time she found no satisfaction in it.

'I'm sorry,' he muttered. 'I wasn't trying to hurt you. I just want you to talk to me, tell me what's wrong.'

Brooke genuinely wished that she could, because the thought of his loving Francesca was eating her up alive. She could have borne his having had an affair with her. Like Giuseppe said, that would now have been past history. But to be in love with her. To have been in love with her all these years!

It was inevitable that one day soon she would have to broach the subject of Francesca. But not now. Now was not the right time at all. The children would be back soon, and she had no intention of arguing in front of them.

Thinking of the children brought some sanity back to her troubled soul.

'Leo…please…just leave it for now.'

'No,' he said stubbornly. 'You're angry with me for some reason and I don't know why.'

'I guess that's the problem, Leo,' she said wearily. 'You don't know why...'

'You're talking in riddles, woman!'

It was the wrong thing for him to say.

'Don't you dare call me that,' she snapped once more. 'My name is Brooke. Brooke! Brooke! Brooke! I'm not *woman*.'

'Oh, I see,' he sneered back. 'This is some kind of feminist issue. *That's* why you want to go running to your darling mother. So what is it, Brooke? You're dissatisfied with just being a wife and mother now, is that it? You want more? You want a career, maybe? Or is it *me* you're dissatisfied with? I haven't been giving you enough of the sex you suddenly seem to want? If that's the problem, sweetheart, then believe me, I'm your man. You don't honestly think I've been all that thrilled with the way things have been going in bed this last year, do you? There's just so many faked orgasms a husband can endure before he starts looking elsewhere.'

Brooke stared at him, stunned by his attack, *furious* that he would use such a feeble excuse for his unfaithfulness. Okay, so she *had* faked a few orgasms the past year or two. Wasn't that better than just saying, no, she didn't feel like it, thank you very much, come back another night? At least *he'd* been satisfied. He'd certainly rolled over straight away afterwards and gone to sleep in seconds.

She was opening her mouth to point this out to him when Claudia ran into the kitchen. 'Mummy, I'm all clean now,' she said, tugging at her mother's skirt again. 'I want some Coco Pops and juice.'

Brooke bent down and picked her up, summoning up a smile from wherever mothers summoned up smiles, even when their hearts were breaking. 'Then we'd better get you some Coco Pops and juice *pronto*, hadn't we?' Thank heavens for long-life products, she thought, since they'd hardly had time to do any food shopping since getting off the plane.

'And I suppose we'd better get Daddy his coffee before he has a hernia,' she added ruefully.

'What's a hernia?' Alessandro chirped as he ran into the kitchen.

'What I'm already having,' Leo muttered, his voice clipped and cold. 'You can forget the coffee for now. I'm going down to our bedroom to ring my parents, let them know we've arrived safely.'

'Fine,' Brooke said, infinitely glad to have him out of the room.

By the time he reappeared, some considerable time later, she had herself temporarily under control. Though for how long, she could only guess.

'I won't leave to go to my mother's till the children are asleep,' she told him tautly as she made his coffee. 'They shouldn't be any trouble.'

He stood in the doorway, watching her. 'Brooke, you have to tell me what's bothering you.'

'Yes. Yes, I know,' she admitted. 'Just not now.'

'Why not now? We're alone.'

Which they were. The children had finished breakfast and were at that moment watching some children's programme on television in the rumpus room. Even Alessandro was content to sit quietly this morning, as he was tired. Brooke could see they wouldn't last too long before it was nap-time.

'When, then?'

'Tonight. When the children have gone to bed.'

'Tonight, then,' Leo agreed reluctantly, and Brooke let out a ragged sigh.

CHAPTER SIX

It was a mistake to come here, Brooke thought as she finished pouring out the whole sorry story. The expression on her mother's face said it all. The *I told you so*s were about to start.

'What a bastard!' Phyllis bit out. 'And there I was, utterly convinced Leo was different, that he loved you almost as much as you loved him, that he was a darned good husband and father and nothing like the lying, cheating creeps I had the misfortune to marry. I was almost convinced I'd been wrong about the male species in general. I even started looking favourably at a certain member of the male species I met recently.'

Brooke was speechless. Her mother…looking favourably at a *man*?

'But it turns out darling Leo was just a little cleverer than most men in getting what he wanted,' her mother swept on scornfully, bringing Brooke's mind back from this new mystery man to the man who mattered.

Brooke found herself bristling at her mother's hasty condemnation of Leo. It smacked of a bias and bitterness which was only too ready to jump to the worst conclusions, *never* giving the benefit of the doubt.

'And what, exactly, did Leo want, Mum?' Brooke challenged in brittle tones.

'A beautiful wife who adored him enough to stay home and play full-time housewife and mother, giving him free rein to do exactly what he wanted to do, when he wanted to do it, no questions asked.'

'That's hardly fair. I *chose* to be a full-time house-wife and mother.'

'Did you indeed? I thought you told me once you wanted to go back to work. But I dare say Leo vetoed *that* idea quick-smart. He wouldn't have wanted his beautiful wife out there in the big, bad world. Meanwhile, *he's* out there, having any woman who takes his fancy, including his brother's widow. Oh, yes, don't go doubting him on *that* score. He went to bed with Francesca all right. Men are never to be trusted, Brooke, especially where sex is concerned. Conniving, deceitful, selfish, uncaring bastards, every one of them! I thank you for reminding me.

'Hell, I need a cigarette,' she muttered, and snatched up the unopened packet lying in the centre of the garden table, ripping off the Cellophane and extracting a cigarette with shaking hands. 'Damn, I left my lighter inside. Won't be a moment.'

Brooke just sat there, frowning. How strange, she was thinking. Her mother had only been saying what she herself had been thinking and fearing, but coming from someone else it just didn't sound right. It didn't sound like Leo.

Leo *wasn't* conniving, or deceitful, or uncaring. A little selfish, maybe. But that *was* the nature of the beast. In the main, he was very considerate towards her and the children.

'I've been trying to give up smoking,' her mother snapped on her return.

Brooke blinked her surprise. Her mother had been

smoking sixty cigarettes a day for as long as she could remember. Her even *trying* to give them up was unheard of.

'For this *man*, would you believe? I even went out and had my roots dyed blonde,' she raged on between prolonged puffs.

Brooke's startled eyes jerked up to her mother's hair. Good Lord, she *had*, too.

'Well, it looks good, Mum,' she said truthfully. 'In fact, you're looking darned good all round. Put on a few pounds, haven't you?'

'That's from giving up smoking. I was even going to ask you to help me with my make-up and wardrobe this week. But not now. God, what a fool I've been!' Scowling, she dragged in deeply on the cigarette. 'And what a fool *you've* been,' she directed waspishly at Brooke. 'I warned you Leo would make you miserable. And I was right!'

'You were *wrong*!' Brooke countered. Leaning over, she snatched the cigarette out her mother's startled hand and stabbed it to death in the till then amazingly empty ashtray. 'Leo's made me very happy. He's a wonderful husband and a wonderful father. Please don't use this small personal crisis of mine as an excuse to wallow in old bitternesses, or to start smoking again!'

Phyllis made a scoffing sound. '"Small personal crisis" indeed. Your husband doesn't *love* you, Brooke. He's just *used* you.'

'Don't be such a drama queen, Mum. Leo does love me! He told me so the other night.'

Phyllis shook her head. 'I don't believe I'm hearing this.'

'Well, you are, and you're going to hear more! I've been acting the same way as you, but I can see now how unfair to Leo I've been. I condemned him without a hearing. I was prosecutor, judge and jury. I have no real evidence that he's been unfaithful to me. Or that he's even still in love with Francesca. All I have is gossip and innuendo and suspicion.'

'Are you forgetting the fact he lied to you about where he was that night? And what about the guilty way he crept in? Not to mention the state of his…er…equipment.'

Perversely, the more her mother condemned Leo, the more Brooke felt compelled to defend him. 'Leo explained that. He'd just had a long cold shower.'

Phyllis rolled her eyes. 'For pity's sake, girl, think clearly on this! *Why* didn't Leo tell you he'd once been engaged to Francesca if he no longer loves her?'

'Why should he? That was before he met me. Clearly Leo isn't the type who rakes over the past. If I recall rightly, not once did he ask me about *my* previous boyfriends. And he must have known I'd had at least one! I wasn't a virgin when I met him.'

'Which rather confirms what I said, don't you think?' her mother argued. 'When a man's madly in love with you, he wants to know every single awful detail of every lover you've ever had. I know mine always did. But not Leo, it seems. I wonder why…'

The merciless logic of her mother's argument cut deep. Why *hadn't* Leo asked her about her previous boyfriends?

'I'll tell you why,' Phyllis swept on, before Brooke could think of a single reason. 'Because he didn't care how many men you'd been with. Because he didn't love you. Because he was still in love with Francesca. He only married you because you were pregnant. *And* for the sex.'

Brooke finally saw a chink in her mother's argument and grabbed it. 'I doubt he married me for the sex, Mum. He was *already* getting the sex. And plenty of it. But you're right about one thing. He probably did marry me because I was pregnant. Children *do* seem to mean the world to Italian men. But that doesn't mean Leo didn't love me, or that he was still in love with that stupid Francesca woman. Goodness, she *must* have been stupid to pass up Leo for anyone, especially his brother. Lorenzo was a sleazebag.'

'Sleazebags come in many forms,' Phyllis pointed out. 'Some not so obvious.'

'Leo is no sleazebag. He's a fine man. I'm sorry now that I ever thought he was unfaithful. I should have had more faith in him.'

'Then it would be *blind* faith! So tell me, daughter, what does this Francesca look like? Something tells me she's not ugly.'

Brooke stiffened. 'I won't lie. She's very beautiful.'

'Yet you said Leo hadn't slept with her, despite their engagement. In the past, that is,' came her mother's added tart comment.

'That's right. She was supposed to be a shy virgin back then, and was waiting till their wedding night. Apparently she wasn't so shy once she'd met the sleazebag brother. Leo actually caught them doing it. Did I mention that?'

'No,' Phyllis said, her eyebrows lifting. 'No, you didn't. Which only consolidates what I've been saying. Italian men prize their sexual prowess. Hard for Leo not to take the chance to prove himself the better man once it presented itself...'

Almost despairingly now, Brooke sought reasons not to believe what her mother was saying. 'You're forgetting Francesca in all these suppositions. She does have some say in whom she sleeps with, don't you think? The woman was absolutely besotted by Lorenzo. She was beside herself at his funeral.'

'Maybe. But this Lorenzo's dead, and his widow is undoubtedly very lonely. Do you honestly think she would have been able to resist Leo if he decided to seduce her? Even *I* have to admit that Leo has more sex appeal than any man has a right to.'

'We have no evidence of any such seduction,' Brooke defended staunchly.

'Oh, come now! Leo was *there*, in her apartment! For hours and hours! You told me so!'

Brooke began to get angry, both at her mother, for being so damned smart, and herself, for being so damned stubborn. 'There's loads of reasons why he might have been in Francesca's apartment other than to seduce her. He could have been going through his brother's personal papers.'

'Then why lie about it?'

'I don't know,' she choked out.

'Why, for heaven's sake, don't you just *ask* him?

Why don't you tell him what you overheard as well, and get it all out in the open?'

'Don't you think I've thought of doing just that?' Brooke cried. 'But when did it ever work for you, Mum, confronting your husbands over their sexual behaviour, getting things out in the open? Inevitably it led to bitter arguments, and finally divorce. Once you open that particular Pandora's box, it's impossible to shut it again.'

'You'd really prefer to go on turning a blind eye?' her mother asked, shocked. 'You're happy doing that?'

'I'm not happy at all, Mum. That's why I came over here to talk to you. I had to talk to someone or go stark raving mad. But I have to think of the children's happiness, not just my own silly pride.'

'Yes, of course,' her mother said soberly. 'The children...I'm sorry, Brooke. I'd forgotten about them for a moment. Yes...yes, I see your dilemma.'

'Both Alessandro and Claudia adore Leo. Aside from what might or might not have happened with Francesca, he's a very good father. I don't want a divorce, Mum. I really don't.'

'Then what are you going to do?'

Anguish played across Brooke's face. 'I rather hoped *you* were going to tell me that. I came here desperate for some practical advice, advice that would *save* my marriage, not destroy it.'

'Oh, darling...I'm so sorry...' Phyllis looked both stricken and sympathetic. 'I know how much you love Leo. Too much, I've always thought. But, okay, I'll do my best to help. Just don't jump down my throat if I say things you don't like hearing.'

'I'll try not to.'

'Fair enough. First things first… Let's forget Francesca for a moment, and look at the role *you* chose to play in your marriage. The fact is I never thought you were cut out to be the traditional wife and mother, Brooke, staying at home all the time, bowing to your husband's wishes, stroking *his* ego all the time. Some women can play that part and be perfectly happy with it. But you're much too strong-willed to sustain such an unequal partnership. And much too intelligent.'

Brooke was intrigued by her mother's spot-on observations. But where was she going with this?

'I know you don't see yourself this way, Brooke, but down deep you're a chip off the old block. Your father once told me I was a tiger of a woman, and you're just the same. You *chose* to act like a pussycat in your marriage because you saw what a hopeless mess I made of *my* marriages. But the tiger has escaped now, and I'm afraid you're going to have trouble putting it back into its cage. Now what are you smiling at, daughter? What have I said?'

'That's what Leo called me the other night. A tiger.'

'Mmm. I gather not disparagingly?'

'On, no, he *liked* me being a tiger in bed,' she admitted ruefully.

'Men always like women being tigers in bed. They just don't like it when the tiger doesn't stay there. Look, it probably *would* be better if you could simply ignore what happened in Italy and try to go on as before, but you can't do that now, can you? That's why you're here?'

Brooke nodded.

'I thought as much. I wouldn't be able to, either. So, as a compromise, why don't you start by simply asking Leo about his engagement to Francesca? Say you over-heard someone mention it recently. See what his re-action is.'

Brooke groaned at the thought.

'Don't accuse him of anything further,' her mother went on hastily. 'If you accuse him of adultery and he's guilty he'll just deny it, and your relationship will suffer. If he's innocent he'll be mortally offended, with the same result. It's a no-win situation for a wife.'

Brooke groaned. 'You really think he slept with her, don't you?'

Her mother's eyes carried true sympathy, but her voice was firm. 'There's no use putting your head in the sand, Brooke. You have to admit that, under the circumstances, Leo might have slept with her. But that doesn't mean he loves her. Leo was obviously very happy with *you* when he came home that night. And he said he loved *you.* It's perfectly clear that, whatever happened, he has no intention of leaving you and the children. This Francesca is oceans away. She's hardly an immediate threat to your marriage.'

'You're right,' Brooke said with a burst of well-needed optimism and resolve. 'She's over there and I'm *here*! Frankly, I'd be a fool to even mention her at all. No, I'm going to go home and keep my mouth well and truly shut.' She reached out and took her mother's hand. 'You're a good mum, no matter what you think. And you're not as tough as you make out. Which reminds me... Tell me about this man you've met. He must be something to have you rush off to the hairdresser.'

Brooke could not believe the dreamy look which came into her mother's eyes. 'He's just so gorgeous, Brooke. And only forty-five—two years younger than me. *Very* good-looking. He's a lawyer I met in court. I beat him in a case, actually. Although to be fair his client never stood a chance. I see him quite often around the courts, and he always stops and talks to me. He says I've got a brilliant mind.'

'But it's not your mind you want him to think is brilliant,' Brooke said drily.

Her mother actually blushed. 'I've been so lonely, Brooke. You've no idea.'

'I think I have, Mum. We Freeman women aren't meant for celibacy. We're tigers, both in the bedroom and out. Go get 'im, that's what I say. When do you want to do some clothes-shopping?'

'I'll ring you tomorrow night and we can make a date for later this week. That way I can find out how things are going with Leo.'

'Right.' Brooke jumped to her feet. 'Well, I'd better be going.'

'Aren't you forgetting something, daughter dear?'

Brooke frowned. 'What?'

Phyllis pointed over at the big ginger cat which was at that moment snoozing in the warm autumn sunshine.

Brooke rolled her eyes and slapped her own forehead. 'Lord, I'd forget my head if it wasn't screwed on tight. If I'd gone home without *him*, I'd have been in *real* trouble. Come on, Mister Puss,' Brooke murmured as she scooped him up into her arms, 'time to go home. Time to face the demons.'

CHAPTER SEVEN

IT WAS just after four by the time Brooke turned her navy Falcon into the driveway and eased it into the garage alongside Leo's red Alfa Romeo.

Her mind went to Leo once more on seeing it. Not that it had been far away from her husband during the hour's drive home.

They said you could tell a lot about a man by the kind of car he drove. Leo had chosen the sporty two-seater ostensibly because it was easy to handle in the narrow city streets, and very easy to park. But Brooke knew Leo enjoyed the car's power.

Once, soon after he'd bought it…a few days after they'd met…he'd driven it through the Sydney CBD well over the speed limit, changing lanes like a formula one driver, cornering like a greyhound, racing another car down into the Harbour tunnel and up the other side before spinning round and roaring back into the city across the bridge.

It had been very late on a Monday night—well after midnight—and there'd only been a few other cars on the road, so she supposed it hadn't been as dangerous as it seemed, in retrospect. Still, Brooke had found it a wildly exhilarating and exciting experience, with the top down and her hair streaming out with the wind. When they'd got back to his hotel suite, and Leo had begun undressing her straight away, she'd been as turned on as he was.

She'd chided him breathlessly about his driving while he'd stripped off the last of her underwear, pointing out that if he'd been caught, he would have lost his licence.

'Sometimes,' he'd explained in thickened tones as he'd urged her shockingly naked body across the room and pressed her heated flesh against the large window which overlooked the city streets way below, 'an experience is worth the risk. But don't worry, *mi micetta*,' he'd added, stretching her arms up high above her head and holding her wrists together with a single grasp. 'I'm not a reckless man very often. But why have a fast car without pushing it to the limit at least once?'

His free hand had mercilessly explored her body while he'd watched her breathing become ragged and her lips fall wider and wider apart.

'Much the same could be said for a beautiful woman,' he'd rasped, and had whipped her breathless body round to face the window, releasing her hands to spread them wide and press them, palms down, against the cool glass. She'd dared not move, even when he'd let her hands go, nor protest when he'd eased her legs apart. She had just stood there, quivering with anticipation, while he'd stroked her hair out of the way then kissed her spine from top to bottom, bump by erotic bump.

But he hadn't stopped there; his mouth had moved inexorably downwards...

Brooke's mouth dried at the memory. And at what that night had revealed about Leo.

The truth was her husband could be a reckless man—some might say a *ruthless* man—on occasion. One could conclude that normal moral standards would not stop him seducing a woman if he wanted her badly enough, at least once.

Brooke groaned and buried her face in her hands. During the drive home she'd almost convinced herself that Leo *hadn't* been unfaithful, that he loved *her* and not Francesca. Then she'd seen that car of his and remembered what he was capable of.

The driver's door being wrenched open sent her head jerking up and to the right. Leo stood there, glaring down at her startled and possibly flushed face.

'What in hell are you doing,' he snarled, 'hiding out here in the car? I've been waiting for you to come inside ever since you drove in. What is it now? Can't you even stand to come inside, in case you're alone with me?'

Brooke had not often seen her husband in such a foul temper. In fact it was a rare occurrence.

But he was in a foul temper now.

In the past she might have quailed, then hastened to smooth down his ruffled feathers. Now, his snarls brought out the worst in her: the tiger.

'*Don't* you raise your voice to me,' she said tersely, pushing him back against the garage wall with the car door as she climbed out. 'And don't go thinking about grabbing me again, either,' she warned when she saw the light of battle flare in his eyes. 'I won't stand for any more bully-boy tactics!' she pronounced, and slammed the car door.

Leo fairly spluttered with outrage.

'And I wasn't *hiding* here in the car,' she informed him curtly. 'I was merely getting my thoughts together before I came inside and told you what was *really* bothering me.'

To hell with common sense, she decided angrily. Or turning a blind eye. Or trying to go on as before. She simply *had* to know what Leo felt for Francesca. Everything hinged on that.

'That's what I was trying to find out this morning,' Leo growled. '*Before* you ran off to your mother's and left me with two of the most tiresome, cantankerous, spoiled little brats I've ever encountered in my life!'

Brooke was taken aback, before realising this was the first time, the very first time, that Leo had been left totally alone with his children for longer than a few minutes. She could well imagine that their over-tiredness from the flight, plus her going off to get Mister Puss without them, might have set another cat among the pigeons, so to speak.

She almost smiled, Francesca momentarily forgotten. 'The children misbehaved?'

'That's putting it mildly,' he grumbled.

'But I put them to bed before I left.'

'Maybe so, but they were *not* asleep, and the moment you drove off all hell broke loose. Claudia started crying for some doll she left in Italy. Then Alessandro started whingeing and whining about Mister Puss.'

Suddenly Leo grimaced, and bent towards the back of the car, straightening with a relieved sigh. 'Thank God you didn't forget the cat! If you had, I would have had to take that infernal child over to Turramurra personally! What is it about that animal he finds so damned indispensable?'

'Mister Puss is like a security blanket and motorised soft toy combined. Your son likes to drag him around by his tail and sit on him while he watches his favourite videos.'

'*Don't* talk to me about videos!' Leo snapped. 'When it became obvious that those two little devils were not going to sleep, I let them get up and put the TV back on, at which point my bossy, demanding son informed me that he wanted to watch *The Wiggles in Concert*. Well! Do you think I could find *The Wiggles in Concert*? Not on your life! And nothing else would do!'

'That's his favourite,' Brooke murmured, trying not to laugh.

'Well, where the hell is it hiding? It's not on the shelves with all the other videos.'

'It's probably in his toy box. He watches that one so much it sometimes ends up in there.'

Leo rolled his eyes. 'I never would have thought to look there.'

'Where are the children now?'

'Oh, they're asleep *now*. I finally got them to sleep around two, after I read them a hundred stories. But they're in *our* bed,' he added wryly. 'It was the only way I could settle them down. They thought it was a wonderful treat, since they're not usually allowed in our bedroom.'

Which they weren't.

'I see,' Brooke murmured.

Leo sighed and gave her a rather exhausted look.

'You know, Brooke, this afternoon has made me realise just how difficult a job you have, minding those two all day every day. And yet you never, ever complain about them. You always look fresh and lovely when I come home, the house is tidy and my dinner's all prepared. I can well understand how tired you must feel sometimes, and why you don't feel like sex. But please, Brooke... I don't want you to pretend with me, either in that area or any other. If you don't want me to make love to you, then just say so. If anything else is bothering you, then, please, tell me that too. I want you to be happy,' he said, reaching out to touch her cheek oh, so gently. 'I can't stand it when you're not.'

This was her chance, yet Brooke hesitated. He was being so nice and understanding. So sweet. How could she bring up a subject like Francesca *now*? It would spoil what they *did* have.

'Aren't you happy being married to me any more, Brooke?' he asked, clearly worried by her silence. 'Don't you love me any more?'

'I could ask the same of you, Leo,' she choked out.

'Of *me*?' He looked stunned.

'Yes. Aren't you happy with me any more? Don't you love me...any more?'

If you ever did...

'Are you mad? I'm very happy being married to you. As for loving you... Why, I love you now more than ever!'

Tears filled her eyes. 'Do you, Leo? Do you really?'

With a groan, he pulled her into his arms. 'Where on earth have you been getting such silly ideas? My God, Brooke, I *adore* you. You're my life, you and the children.' He pulled back abruptly and stared down at her. 'Has anyone said anything to you to make you doubt me?'

Oh, if only he knew...

'The thing is, Leo,' she said carefully, 'you've never actually *said* you loved me before, and I...I did over-hear something while we were in Italy which worried me a little.'

He looked stunned. *Appalled.* 'What?' he demanded to know. 'What did you overhear?'

'That...that you were once engaged to Francesca,' she said in a tiny, scared voice.

His face darkened. 'Who was it who said that?'

'Your mother.'

He swore something in Italian, words she'd never heard before.

'Are you saying it's not true?' she asked fearfully. For if he did she would know he was lying.

'No. No, it's true enough,' he confessed, if reluctantly.

Funny. He hadn't lied. But she still didn't feel all that relieved.

'Why didn't you tell me?'

'I didn't want you to know because I thought it might hurt you. That's why I told the family not to ever mention it to you.'

'How could it have hurt me?'

He looked pained. 'Brooke, please...just trust me on this. I love you. I've always loved you.'

'Then why not tell me about Francesca?' she per-sisted. 'Leo, I need a reason for this deception, other-wise I might think really terrible things here.'

He pulled a face. 'Because my engagement to her was so soon before you. I thought you might think... Hell, I didn't want anything to spoil what we had together.'

'How soon was it before me?'

'Must we rake over such ancient history?'

'Yes, Leo, we must.'

He sighed. 'I broke my engagement to Francesca a week before I met you.'

Brooke went white. 'A week. Only a *week*! How could you have been in love with her one week, then me the next?'

'Because I *wasn't* really in love with her. It was nothing more than an infatuation.'

She didn't like that word. Infatuation. It smacked of something uncontrollable. Like an obsession.

Brooke stared at her husband. If he told her the truth about his brother and his fiancée, then maybe she could believe him.

'What led to your engagement breaking up?' she asked, and held her breath.

'My God, what *else* did you overhear?' he exclaimed, his eyes truly troubled. 'Why was my mother gossiping about me and Francesca, anyway, and to whom?'

'She...she was talking to your father. But I moved away and didn't hear any more.' The lie came out swiftly, but was it for her benefit or his? Clearly Leo didn't want to tell her about finding his brother in bed with *his* fiancée. In a way, she could understand that. Leo was a proud man.

'I will speak to Mamma about this,' Leo muttered

angrily. 'I will not have my family making trouble in my marriage where there is none.'

'No, no, Leo, don't say anything. Please, just…just forget about it.'

'But can *you* forget about it? It's clear to me that you've been very troubled by this news. Your tears on the plane. Those strange comments you've been making. Your touchy mood. It's all clear to me now…'

His eyes melted to an expression of incredible sadness and regret. 'How terrible for you to think I married you not loving you, that I might have stood by your side when our son was born not loving you. Let me assure you, Brooke…that's not so. I have *loved* you always, with all my heart. Yes, I'm guilty of not saying so. I have found such words difficult to say in the past. But not any more. I promise. I actually did tell you, you know, after we made love the other night, but you fell asleep and didn't hear me.'

'I…I heard you,' she whispered.

'You—' He broke off, then nodded slowly, sadly. 'You didn't believe me.'

'I didn't know what to think. You hadn't touched me in ages, and when I touched *you* that night, I thought you didn't want me any more.'

'Which was why you pulled out all the stops?'

'Y…yes,' she confessed shakily.

He reached up to run his fingertips over her mouth. 'You're incredible,' he murmured. 'I'll return the favour come Wednesday night, I promise. I presume we *do* have to wait till Wednesday night?' he added ruefully.

She knew what he meant.

'I'm afraid so,' she confirmed, knowing her period would be well finished by then.

'But a kiss or two is not out of the question, is it?'

Brooke gave him her mouth willingly, her heart singing with joy. Leo loved her. He'd always loved her. Francesca was ancient history. It must have been as she'd told her mother. Leo had been going through his brother's papers at his home that day. He just hadn't wanted to say so for fear of starting any gossip. His mother was wrong. Mothers did have a tendency to worry unnecessarily about their children.

Reassured, and full of love for him, Brooke put everything into kissing him back, winding her arms up around his neck and pulling him down hard against her mouth. He responded with a hunger and ardour which literally took her breath away, his tongue thrusting deep into her mouth, echoing what she knew he wanted to do with his body. She could feel his erection against her stomach, his instant arousal bringing Brooke enormous satisfaction.

Whenever his tongue went to withdraw she ensnared the tip between her lips and sucked the whole thing back into her mouth, not wanting him to stop, not wanting the feelings of loving reassurance to end. Only when her own head began spinning did she release him and they both came up for air.

'You're being a wicked little tease, do you know that?' Leo growled, swinging her round and pressing her against the car door.

'You deserve to suffer for making me worry like I did,' she said breathlessly. 'I want you to go on suffering till Wednesday.'

'Is that so?' Casually, he pushed aside her jacket and ran his hands over her soft cashmere top, shaping and kneading her bra-encased breasts till they responded through her clothing, growing full and hard, their nipples aching in their confinement. By the time his hands slid up under the top and took the bra with them Brooke was trembling with desire.

'Leo,' she choked out, half-protest, half-plea.

'Yes, my love?' he drawled, while he did to her nipples what he'd done to them the other night.

'I... I...'

With an abruptness which brought a gasp to her lips, he abandoned her breasts, pulling her bra back to mercilessly enclose and squash their throbbing tips before smoothing down her top and pulling the lapels of her jacket back together.

'And I want *you* to suffer while you wait,' he murmured as he bent to kiss her panting lips. 'I want you so on fire for me come Wednesday night that you won't be capable of faking a single thing. There will be no more secrets between us, my darling wife. And *definitely* no more pretence. From now on when we make love it's going to be real, more real than anything we've ever shared before. *That*, I promise you.'

Suddenly he smiled down at her, his dark eyes dancing with wicked amusement. 'If only I had a camera,' he said. 'I would dearly love to capture that open-mouthed look. Such an incredible mixture of shock and sensuality. It's going to be damned hard to wait. But we will. And the waiting will make it all the better.' He bent to give her one last peck on her stunned lips.

'Now! Let's get this cat out of the car and back into the house before those two little savages wake up.'

Brooke blinked, then dazedly watched her husband coolly set about getting Mister Puss's cage out of the back seat, before making his way from the garage and up the side path towards the front door. She trailed after him, her mouth still open, her nipples still burning.

Leo, however, was striding out confidently, his manner brisk and businesslike. No one would guess that barely a minute before he'd been doing what he'd been doing.

Brooke had always known her husband capable of great self-control when necessary. He prided himself on it. She didn't doubt for a moment it would be *her* who would suffer the most between now and Wednesday. Leo had the distraction of work, for one thing. And he always slept like a log at night, dropping off the moment his head hit the pillow. No tossing and turning for him.

Whereas she…she would think of him all day, every day. Then half the night, every night.

Real, he'd promised. More real than anything they'd shared before…

She wondered what he meant, for surely there was nothing they hadn't shared before. They'd made love in every position *she* knew about.

But then she thought of this new way he'd started playing with her breasts, and she realised there were probably a thousand subtleties and nuances in love-making they'd never tried before. She had to be a babe in the woods in that department compared to Leo.

He'd been thirty-two when she'd met him, a handsome, sophisticated, wealthy man, who'd travelled widely and, yes, been around. Just because he hadn't slept with Francesca it didn't mean he hadn't had hundreds of other very experienced women, whereas she… She had had less than a handful of boyfriends before Leo, all young men with more bravado than technique.

That was why Leo had blown her away in bed. He'd done things to her and made her do things to him which at the time had seemed incredibly exciting. But maybe—on a rating of one to ten—their lovemaking so far had never got above a five. Maybe there was a lot more. Maybe he was going to show her six to ten on Wednesday night.

Brooke choked out a small sound and Leo, who'd been walking on ahead of her, halted and glared over his shoulder at her. 'What *now*?' he said.

Her heart skipped a beat. 'I didn't say a word.'

'I'm sure I heard you say something.'

'It was nothing. Nothing at all!'

His eyes narrowed. 'I thought I said no more secrets.'

'Come Wednesday night,' she reminded him, smiling nervously.

The corner of his absolutely gorgeous mouth curved up slightly. 'All right. You can have a reprieve till then. But come Wednesday night you're going to tell me everything that's been going on in that surprisingly complex mind of yours. You're going to expose your very soul to me, Brooke, before I'm finished.'

Brooke's insides quivered.

She imagined she would.

And quite a bit else too!

CHAPTER EIGHT

COME seven-thirty Wednesday night, Brooke was hopelessly excited, and even more hopelessly nervous.

Leo had rung that morning from work and told her that his plans for their anniversary night had changed and now required her to pack a small overnight bag, since they would not be returning home till the morning.

'Please do not find any objections,' he'd added swiftly. 'I have already made arrangements to have the children minded.'

Brooke had been thrilled, but also slightly worried. The nanny service they used for evenings out *was* very reputable and reliable, but she'd never left the children with anyone overnight before, except her mother.

When she'd mentioned this, Leo had startled her with the added announcement that it was her mother who was going to mind them. He'd just spoken to her by phone and she would be coming straight to their place after she'd finished at the office that day. Brooke was to expect her no later than six, in time to help her get the children bathed, fed and in bed, and for Brooke to then get ready in peace.

Leo had added that he himself would be dressing away from home and would pick her up right on eight. She was to be wearing her red velvet dress, sheer stay-up stockings, strappy gold sandals...

And nothing else.

'*Nothing* else?' she'd repeated, her stomach curling over.

'Make-up and perfume would be acceptable,' he'd drawled.

'But…but…'

'Nothing else, Brooke. Not a damned thing. Not even jewellery.'

She'd quivered all over. 'What about my hair?'

'Put it up, out of the way.'

'Out of the way of what?'

'*Me.*'

She'd begun to go to mush when she'd suddenly pulled herself up. She was doing it again. Losing her will-power. Letting Leo run the show entirely. Letting him run *her*.

'I'll do it, Leo,' she said, managing to find a cool voice from somewhere. Darned difficult when she was in imminent danger of a sexually charged meltdown. 'But only because *I* want to. Only because the thought of being naked under my clothes excites the hell out of me.'

'Mmm. Have I unleashed the tiger again, *mi micetta*?'

'In more ways than you could possibly imagine.'

He laughed. He actually laughed. 'I will look forward to tonight even more than before,' he'd said. 'See you right on eight.' And he'd hung up.

Such false bravado, Brooke thought now, as she glanced down at the meagre amount of clothes laid out on her bedspread. Whatever had possessed her to agree to going out with no panties on? Being braless was bad enough in that particular dress.

It was made in a new kind of stretch velvet which clung like a second skin. Any modesty in its styling— it had a not too deep round neckline, long sleeves and a hemline just a few inches above her knees—would be negated by her lack of underwear. She might as well walk around naked.

At least you won't have to worry about panty lines or straps showing, she told herself drily, trying to re-capture the tiger in her. But it was asleep in its cage at that moment. She was back to being a kitten again, nervy and ready for flight.

Except there was nowhere to run to. Leo would be arriving in less than half an hour. Thank heavens she'd already done her hair and make-up. Still, she would have to get a wriggle on—wriggle being the operative word. You *had* to wriggle to pull that darned dress on. She'd only worn it once, to a dinner party in Milan, *with* underwear. Even so, Lorenzo's lewd eyes had been on her all night.

It hadn't seen the light of day since.

Sitting down on the side of the bed with a sigh, Brooke reached for the stay-up stockings first, the ones she'd had to dash down to the mall this afternoon to buy. It was a struggle pulling them on and getting them high enough. There was a lot of Lycra in them. Finally she snapped the lacy tops into place, just above mid-thigh. Slipping off her robe, she stood up and walked over to the cheval mirror in the corner.

'Oh, dear heaven!' she gasped when she saw herself. Leo had been right. There was something incredibly

sexy about stocking-encased legs when everything else
was nude. It was even turning *her* on. She would look
even more wicked with her high heels on, Brooke realised, and let out a long, shuddering breath.

She couldn't take her eyes off her erotic reflection,
trying to see it through Leo's eyes. Her hands lifted to
travel shakily down over her breasts, her ribs, her stomach. She still had a darned good figure, even if her full
breasts had settled a little lower on her chest. Her stomach was flat and her bottom still pert. She'd been so
lucky not to get stretch marks during her pregnancies,
and naturally—good little wife that she was—she'd
done all the exercises she was supposed to do afterwards, all the sit-ups, pelvic floor tightenings and what-
nots, so that she'd got her figure back not just outside
but inside as well.

'Brooke!' her mother suddenly called through the
door. 'It's ten to eight. Are you nearly ready?'

'Won't be long!' she called back, snatching up her
robe and holding it nervously in front of her nakedness.

'Shake a leg, then. You don't want to keep Leo waiting, do you?'

Thankfully, her mother didn't come in. Once she'd
gone, Brooke threw aside the robe and snatched up the
dreaded dress, stepping swiftly into it, then wriggling
frantically as she drew it up over her hips. Once there,
she slid her arms into the long, tight sleeves before
hauling it up onto her shoulders, then, doing contor-
tions as only women can do, she zipped the back up
to her neck.

That done, she straightened, smoothed the dress back

down where it had bunched up, and finally dared to glance at herself in the mirror.

Oh, dear God, she thought as she stared at her nipples. They were standing out like nails, open testimony to both her braless and highly aroused state.

As for the rest of her... Okay, so no one would *know* she was naked downstairs, not in this age of G-strings and pantyhose, but she herself was shockingly aware of being naked above and between her stocking-clad thighs. When she walked over to slide her feet into her gold sandals, the silk lining of the dress slid seductively over her nude buttocks. When she sat on the side of the bed to do up the ankle straps on her shoes, it stuck to her like glue.

Leo was a devious and knowing devil, she realised. He knew exactly how dressing like this would affect her.

Once the straps were buckled properly, she stood up and walked gingerly over to the mirror once more, where she stared at the image she presented, at the sexy red dress and the even sexier gold shoes, at the blush in her cheeks and the glittering in her dilated blue eyes. Even her hairstyle was sexy. Though up, it wasn't scraped back tightly, just wound into a loose-ish knot, with bits and pieces left to feather softly around her face.

She looked like a woman just made love to, and expecting to be made love to some more any second. She didn't look like a whore, exactly, but she didn't look like a wife. She looked like some rich man's mistress.

Coward that she was, Brooke left it till the last second before emerging. Thankfully, by this time, the children were safely in bed and sound asleep, and her mother was watching television.

Phyllis glanced up when Brooke walked a little stiffly into the living room, and whistled.

'Mum, *really*,' Brooke said, blushing furiously.

'No, really, darling, you look stunning. And soooo sexy! Remind me to buy something in red when we go shopping together. Remember, you promised to go clothes-shopping with me this week some time?'

'Oh, dear, I *had* forgotten. You should have reminded me when I rang on Monday.'

'Well, we had more interesting things to talk about that day, didn't we? All that good news about Leo and the dreaded Francesca. I was so relieved, I can tell you. I was sick with worry when you left on Sunday. But Leo has restored my faith in men. Which is just as well, because I don't think I could have resisted Matthew much longer. Next time he asks me out, I'm going to say yes. So, could we take the children down to the mall after you get home in the morning and see what we can find? I'm sure to see Matthew again this Friday, and if I can look even a quarter as good as you do tonight, I'll have him lying in the corridor with his tongue hanging out.'

'Shouldn't you wait till you're behind closed doors?' Brooke said with a straight face, though inside she was smiling. She hadn't seen her mother this happy in years.

Both women looked at each other and laughed…till the sound of the doorbell interrupted them.

'That will be Leo,' she said in almost hushed tones, her stomach instantly swirling.

Her mother gave her a stern look. 'None of that doormat nonsense, daughter dear. You're no pussycat any more. Look at yourself. You're a tiger! Let him hear you roar.'

The doorbell rang again, a very lengthy ring.

Now Brooke hurried to the door, because if he kept that up, the children might wake!

Yanking the door open, she was about to chide Leo for being so impatient and thoughtless when the words died in her throat.

Her husband was standing there looking utterly gorgeous. Even more handsome and stylish than usual, if that were possible.

He always looked fantastic, his grooming and fashion sense impeccable. But tonight he'd outdone himself. His sleek black hair lay in perfect symmetry around his well-shaped head and there was not a hint of five-o'clock shadow on his chin. He must have showered and shaved again somewhere, not long ago. Where? she wondered momentarily.

But it was his choice of clothes which drew her eye, all obviously new, since she hadn't seen them before. His suit looked the latest in Italian fashion, coal-black in colour, and not padded in its tailoring, allowing his own marvellous shape to fill out the shoulders of the single-breasted jacket. His shirt was the palest grey and collarless, with small grey pearl buttons done right up to his tanned throat.

When he lifted his hand off the doorbell, his black

onyx and diamond-encrusted dress ring sparkled under the porch light.

'I see the ban on jewellery didn't extend to yourself,' she murmured, smiling. 'And, if I'm not mistaken, they are brand-new clothes you're wearing.'

'I told you I was going to pull out all the stops tonight.' His sexily hooded gaze drank her in for a few smouldering seconds during which Brooke found it difficult to keep standing up straight.

'You look incredible,' he murmured. 'Did you do what I asked?'

She tried to look cool, but it was impossible with him looking at her like that.

He smiled. 'I see by your face that you did.'

'It *feels* wicked,' she whispered, and he laughed softly.

'That's how it's meant to feel. Shall we go, Signora Parini?' he said, picking up the overnight bag she'd placed at the ready by the front door.

Taking a deep breath, she resolved to match his sophistication and insouciance.

'And where are we going to, Signor Parini?'

'Down memory lane. But with a difference.'

'Sounds intriguing. I just have to get my purse,' she told him. 'It's on the hall stand, alongside the beautiful red roses you sent me. I put them there, where I can admire them every time I walk past.'

'And I put your lovely lady on my desk, where I can admire it and think of you every time I look at it.'

First thing this morning Brooke had given him a carving in wood of an elegant lady with long hair. She'd found out from a book that on a five-year anniversary you gave gifts in wood. Leo had given her the longest kiss after opening his present, and told her she would have to wait for her two presents. The first had been the flowers; the second was still to make an appearance.

Obviously he meant to give it to her some time during the evening. Brooke had tried to imagine what it was, but was at a loss. Leo hadn't been all that imaginative a present-giver over the years. He usually resorted to the standbys of perfume and chocolates.

Her mother came out into the hall when they both walked back in.

'My, my,' she said admiringly. 'Don't you two look simply splendid together? Have a wonderful night, darlings. And, Leo...'

'Yes, Phyllis?'

'Don't forget what I told you about the wine.'

'I won't. Don't worry.'

'Mum told *you* something about wine?' Brooke said with surprise in her voice as they walked together out to the red Alfa Romeo waiting at the kerb.

Leo slung Brooke's small bag onto the back seat, a rueful smile on his face.

'She certainly did,' he drawled.

'I can't imagine what. There's nothing you don't know about wine, and Mum is a bit of a Philistine in that department.'

'I doubt that very much. Your mum is a very experienced and intelligent lady. And far more sensible than I ever gave her credit for. Far more sensitive too, I'll warrant. We should visit her more often.'

'Goodness! What brought this on?'

'Let's just say I've realised Phyllis and I have much more in common than I realised.'

'What?' Brooke said laughingly. 'Wine?'

'No, my darling. Our love for you,' he said, and, taking her right hand, he lifted it slowly to his mouth like a Latin lover, narrowed eyes lifted to hers from under his dark brows as his lips made contact with her suddenly trembling fingers.

Brooke had never known what women saw in this type of kissing, or why it should turn their knees to jelly. But as Leo's eyes held hers, and his lips travelled over the back of her hand with a series of feather-like kisses, tingles ran up and down her spine and darts of fire shot between her thighs, reminding her hotly that she was naked there, naked and more than ready for him. Already.

'Is…is this your idea of making me suffer some more?' she choked out.

'Some *more*, my love? Does that mean you've actually *been* suffering?'

'You know I have,' she rasped, and went to pull her hand away. But he held it tight.

'Then that makes two of us, my sweet,' he said. 'But a little erotic torment won't kill us. It will only make everything better in the end. Trust me.'

With that, he helped her down into the low-slung leather seat.

Brooke almost panicked when her tight skirt rode up dangerously high, showing all of her lace-topped stockings and an inch or two of thigh. Brooke glanced up as she wriggled it back down.

Leo smiled a rueful smile, shut the car door and strode round towards the driver's side.

'I have to confess, however,' he drawled as he climbed in behind the wheel, 'that I'm glad I didn't go with my original idea for a chauffeur-driven car and dinner somewhere. The thought of sitting with you as you are at this moment in the back of some roomy limousine while someone else did the driving would have been my undoing. Much better that I have my hands firmly on the wheel and my eyes on the road ahead.' With that, he gunned the Alfa's throaty engine and sped off in the direction of the city.

Brooke decided some distracting conversation would serve them both. She'd never felt this turned on in all her life!

'So, we're heading into the big smoke, are we?' she said brightly.

Leo shrugged. 'I guess there's no point in my keeping it a secret any longer. I'm taking you to the Majestic for the night, to our old suite.'

'Oh, Leo. How romantic!'

He slanted a warm smile her way. 'I hoped you'd think that. Unfortunately it won't look quite the same. They've just refurbished all the rooms. I read about it in the paper over morning coffee and decided on the spot that that was where I wanted to take you. It seemed…appropriate. After all, we did spend our wedding night there.'

'Not to mention just about every night over the previous two months,' Brooke said, smiling at him. Leo could not be taking her anywhere better. She'd been so happy during that time. The place would have wonderful vibes for her. 'But you're not going to drive like you did one night back then, I hope?' she added teasingly.

'Ah. You still remember that night?'

'How could I forget it?'

For some reason he fell broodingly silent after that remark, and she wondered why?

'Did I say something wrong, Leo?' she asked tentatively.

His frown cleared instantly and he threw her a reassuring smile. 'You? You never say anything wrong. I was just off in another world for a moment. Look, I read about something else in the paper this morning too. Something which interested me very much and which I'd like to discuss with you.'

'Oh? What?'

'Firstly, tell me where you think I bought the clothes I'm wearing tonight?'

Brooke blinked her surprise but gave his clothes a second look. 'Well…ummm…they're definitely Italian in design. They have that look about them. And I know you, Leo. Only the best for you when it comes to clothes. But to be honest I can't quite place the style. Not Armani. Or Gucci. Definitely not Brioni. No…I don't know. I give up. You'll have to tell me.'

'It's Orsini.'

'Sorry. I don't know that label. Is it new?'

'Very. But it's about to go out of business.'

'What? But why? Their clothes are wonderful.'

'Lack of money, basically. And the state of the economy. Times are very tough for all the Australian fashion houses at the moment.'

Brooke frowned. 'But I thought we were talking about an Italian fashion house.'

'No. The owner's an Australian/Italian named Vince Orsini. His parents migrated thirty years ago. He's twenty-seven, born and bred in Sydney. He studied design at college here, and with the help of a loan and a small inheritance started up a business in Surry Hills a few years back. But he never had enough for decent advertising and promotion, and now he's going under. There was an article about him in this morning's paper, on the same page as the story about the Majestic's makeover. I was impressed by his obvious passion for fashion, and went to see him.'

'Today!' Brooke was startled.

'Yes, today. I bought this outfit this afternoon for a fraction of what I would have been prepared to pay for it. It made me think that wealthy people all over the world would pay heaps for Vince's clothes too, if only they knew about them, so I offered him a deal. I'd back him financially and we'd go into partnership.'

Brooke was stunned. 'But, Leo…fashion is a long way from furniture and household products.'

He smiled wryly. 'You don't think I can make a success of it?'

'I think you would make a success of anything you did.'

His smile widened. 'I'd hoped you say that. I've worked for my father long enough, Brooke. I have enough money now to strike out on my own. I inherited a substantial sum from my grandmother's estate when I was twenty-five and invested it rather well, even if I say so myself. There's more than enough now to take a chance without bankrupting us, whether the idea succeeds or fails. Parini's won't suffer by my defection. It's a long-established company, with good managers and staff in all its branches. I know exactly the man to put in charge in Sydney. He'll do an excellent job.'

'But what will your father say?'

Leo shrugged. 'I have to be my own man. If he wants me to, I'll keep a personal eye on things for him, play troubleshooter if and when needed. But the rest of the time I want to do something else, something more…challenging.'

'I know what you mean,' she said. 'It's not good to be bored with your job.'

He slid thoughtful eyes her way. 'Which brings me to my next idea…'

'What's that?'

'I want you to help me in this project.'

Brooke could not have been more startled, or more pleased. She'd wanted to go back to work some time. 'In what way?'

'In *every* way. Vince designs women's clothes as well as men's. With your looks and style and intelligence, you'd be perfect to head the PR department in the women's wear section while I do the men's. I've been thinking we could take the collection to Milan each year. I have plenty of business connections over there. You speak Italian like a native, so there's no problem there. And then there's Tokyo.'

'Tokyo!'

'Yes. They're crazy for fashion there, yet they've been neglected by the world at large in that area. I'm sure Orsini's would be a great success in Asia. Of course, I haven't forgotten that you speak Japanese like a native too.'

'I'm pretty rusty on the Japanese, Leo.'

'You'll pick it up again. You're so clever with languages. So what do you think?'

'You've taken my breath away.'

'But you like the idea?'

'I *love* the idea. But…'

'I know exactly what you're going to say. But what about the children. Look, there's no need for you to work full-time to begin with. And a lot can be done from home, you know, with the right electronic equipment. Of course, you *are* going to need extra help in the home, so I rang Italy a little while ago and asked Nina if she'd like to come to Australia and work for us.'

Brooke could not believe Leo had done all this in one day! But it seemed to agree with him. It wasn't just clothes making the man tonight, she realised. It was his energy and his enthusiasm. In a way he reminded her of her mother. He was totally revitalised and absolutely bursting with life.

'So what did Nina say?' she asked. But she could guess. Who could say no to Leo in this mood?

He grinned. 'She can't wait. Said she could be on the next plane.'

'But where will she sleep?'

'I realised that needed addressing. But Rome wasn't built in a day, Brooke, and this project won't get off the ground for a while. Vince has to honour a couple of his present contracts first. So I told Nina she won't be needed for at least three months. Then I contacted our old renovators over lunch and gave them the job of building a small flat over the double garage. They said they could do that for me in *two* months. Easy. Which means it might be done in three.'

'My goodness, Leo, what a busy boy you've been today!'

'You don't know the half of it. Damn, just look at this traffic. It should have cleared by now. I've booked our table in the hotel restaurant for eight-thirty, but at this rate we'll be late.'

'Let's skip the fancy dinner, Leo. If you're really hungry you can order something to be served in the room.'

'You really wouldn't mind?' He flashed her a dazzling smile and she just wanted to kiss him. Right at that moment. When they pulled up at a red light, she leant over and did just that.

'All I have on my menu tonight, Leo,' she murmured against his mouth, 'is you...'

He swore. In Italian. When Leo was really rattled, he dropped into Italian.

'I think you should stop being a tiger and go back to being a kitten,' he grated out. 'At least till we get to the hotel.'

The light turned green just as Brooke laid a provocative hand on Leo's thigh and began to slide it up his trouser leg. When the Alfa Romeo shot abruptly forward she fell back into her seat, laughing.

'I've had about enough of this,' Leo growled, and, whisking the car into another lane with barely inches to spare, he set about making her heart race even faster than it already was.

Brooke was grateful the top wasn't down. Beside being far too cold, her upswept hairdo would not have lasted a minute.

CHAPTER NINE

LEO wasn't as reckless as on that previous occasion over five years ago. Impossible, with the traffic as heavy as it was. Neither did he really speed. But he drove with purpose, using every opportunity to save a few seconds here, a minute there, taking backstreets and shortcuts till they were soon in the inner city and heading for the Majestic.

Brooke could see their destination a few blocks away, rising tall and, yes, majestically above the bulk of the city skyline, although it wasn't quite as tall as the Centrepoint Tower. But the Majestic was almost as high, and circular in shape, a very modern concrete and glass structure, both in architecture and decor.

Brooke could not imagine why the owners of the hotel had felt they needed to refurbish the rooms, but she supposed things did get a little shabby after a while with constant use.

Leo muttered, 'At last,' as he zapped into the Majestic's semi-circular driveway, coming to an impatient halt beside the huge revolving glass doors which steered the hotel's patrons inside its spacious foyer.

Once the engine was cut, Leo swiftly recomposed himself, alighting to hand the valet-parking attendant his keys with his usual smooth panache. Meanwhile the doorman had opened the car door for her, and was about to help her out when Leo intervened.

'I'll do that,' he said, and instructed the doorman to get the overnight bag from behind the seats and send it up to his suite. 'Parini's the name,' he said, before returning his attention to Brooke.

Leo was a stickler for manners of the gallant kind. When she went out with him, Brooke always felt like a queen. Tonight she felt like a sex goddess as well as he drew her out of the car and onto the wide pavement, his darkly smouldering eyes sending prickles of desire rippling down her spine.

'I'm so glad you decided against dinner in public,' he whispered as he guided her into the revolving doors, pressing himself tellingly against her backside. 'The thought of other men enjoying you tonight in any way whatsoever, even vicariously, is simply not on. You are for my eyes only this evening, my love. And for the rest of our lives together.'

Brooke could not help thrilling to his impassioned words, even if he did sound a little over-possessive. But she would forgive him anything tonight.

Tonight was not quite real, she accepted, despite Leo saying the other day it would be. He was bringing a romantic fantasy to life here, recreating the time when they had just met, when Leo had been the dominant erotic master and she his willing love-slave.

But, whilst it had been wonderful at the time, Brooke knew she didn't want that kind of relationship with Leo any more. She wanted a true partnership with him, in the bedroom as well as out of it. Undoubtedly he was beginning to understand that, since he'd already soft-

ened his chauvinistic stance with his offer to her of
being involved in this fashion project.

But in truth she wanted more from him than just that.
She wanted to be Leo's best friend as well as his wife
and business partner. She wanted to be his confidante,
she wanted *emotional* intimacy, not just of the physical
kind.

But these changes could not happen overnight,
Brooke realised. And certainly not tonight.

Tonight she would be generous and giving and not
make an issue of things. To be honest, it was still very
exciting to surrender herself to Leo's will sexually. She
just didn't want to have to do it all the time. She
wanted the right to say no when she really didn't feel
like it, and she wanted the right to take the initiative
sometimes.

Brooke hung back a little while Leo collected his
key from Reception and ordered some food to be sent
up to their room as soon as possible, during which time
Brooke tried not to mind the way the attractive redhead
behind the desk immediately began making eyes at her
husband.

The girl was very lovely, however, and Leo was taking longer than necessary, she thought. Jealousy sent
her fingers clutching tighter around her gold evening
purse, and she was about to explode when a man in a
pinstriped suit materialised by her side and tried the
old line of didn't he know her from somewhere?

She dispensed with him with a coldly furious glare
just as Leo turned away from the desk. Frowning, he
hurried back to take her elbow and usher her towards
the bank of lifts.

'I leave you alone for one miserable minute,' he growled, 'and the dogs start sniffing around.'

Brooke bristled at this highly unfair remark.

'Really?' she snapped. 'Well, you'll just have to learn to live with it, Leo, if you want to take me out dressed like this! *I* have to put up with the way women fawn over *you* all the time. The moment you get within three feet of them they begin acting like bitches in heat! If they were on four legs instead of two they'd be wagging their little tushies in your face. As it is, they flutter their eyelashes and smile so much it's a wonder their lips don't set that way, like the Joker in Batman!'

Leo ground to a halt and just stared at her.

Brooke stared right back, angry and unrepentant.

The corner of Leo's mouth eventually lifted into a slow, wry smile. 'Your mother was right,' he said ruefully. 'I have no idea what I've married. But I'm finding out. Come along, tiger woman,' he ground out. 'Sheathe those claws for a while, till we can put them to better use.'

Unfortunately there were other people in the lift riding up, so Brooke could not ask exactly what it was her mother had been saying about her. But she could guess. Her mother must have warned Leo that change was in the air and that he'd better be prepared to go along with things or there'd be trouble in the camp.

And she was darned right!

Brooke smiled as she recalled the exhilaration which had raced through her as she'd let rip just now. Boy, it had felt great letting off steam like that.

'What on earth are you smiling at?' Leo asked as he walked her along to the door of their old suite.

Brooke eyed her wary-sounding husband with renewed confidence. 'Ah…now that's for me to know
and you to find out. Later,' she added mischievously,
stretching up to give him a provocative lick on his lips.

His eyes gleamed, and he might have grabbed her
right then and there if a uniformed waiter hadn't been
wheeling a trolley down the corridor towards them.

When he stopped right next to them and said, 'Room
service for Mr Parini,' Brooke blinked her surprise.

'Wow,' she muttered under her breath. 'Now *that*
was quick!'

'As agreed,' Leo pronounced, and handed the youth
a hundred-dollar note. 'Don't worry about setting it up
inside,' he said. 'We'll do that.'

The waiter beamed. 'Thank *you*, sir. If there's anything else you require further during the evening, don't
hesitate to ring.' He grinned and sauntered off, whis-
tling.

'You gave him a hundred-dollar tip!' Brooke exclaimed, stunned. No one tipped that high in Sydney.
It just wasn't expected.

'Amazing what the right financial incentive will do.
They told me there would be a half-hour delay in the
room service, so I spoke to the kitchen personally and
said there would be a hundred dollars for whoever got
the food to my room within five minutes. Not that they
had to cook anything. I ordered seafood and salad,
champagne and strawberries.'

Opening the door, Leo waved her inside while he
followed with the trolley.

'So, basically, you subscribe to the same theory as

your father,' Brooke pointed out as she walked in and glanced around the redone rooms with curious eyes.

They'd certainly gone to town on a grand scale, opting for an extremely rich, modern look rather than the cosy country decor of before. The colour scheme was now black and grey and white, instead of blues and greens, with all clean lines and solid colours. Not a hint of floral or stripes anywhere. The carpet was plush grey, the walls white, and the furniture expensive squashy black leather.

'What theory is that?' Leo asked as he wheeled the trolley past the archway which led into the kitchen—a dauntingly modern vision in black marble and stainless steel. He stopped next to the large black sofa which ran along one wall of the sitting area. A long, low glass and black wrought-iron coffee table stood on the black and white rug in front of it, opposite which stood a huge grey-painted entertainment unit, which housed a television, video and hi-fi arrangement, complete with complimentary CDs.

'That money can buy you anything,' Brooke replied, and wandered over to stand at the floor-to-ceiling window where once she'd surrendered to the most erotic experience in her life. It still had the same view, of the Harbour and the Opera House, and whilst the glass was tinted, and too high up for anyone on the city streets below to see anything, she still felt slightly exposed standing next to it.

'Money *can* buy you any *thing*, Brooke. It just can't buy you intangible things, such as love or talent or happiness. It can, however, buy you some damned fine food and the very best French champagne.'

She glanced over her shoulder at him, just as he whisked the covering cloth off the trolley to reveal a mouthwatering array of dishes, plus not one but *two* bottles of champagne, chilling in individual silver ice buckets.

Suddenly the penny dropped with regard to her mother's earlier comment about the wine. She'd told Leo to buy champagne.

Brooke had always been very partial—and susceptible—to champagne, right from her eighteenth birthday, when a friend of the family had bought her a magnum and she'd drunk most of it. She'd had the time of her life. And so had her boyfriend at the time, she'd gathered the next day.

'Are you sure you haven't ordered too much champagne, Leo?' she said cheekily as she sashayed back towards him. 'After all, my limit when I'm with you is two glasses.'

Leo sighed. 'Now, Brooke, about that...'

'Yes, Leo?'

'I'm sorry I took it upon myself to tell you what to drink and how much to drink. It was wrong of me. My only excuse is that I noticed you became somewhat...er...flirtatious when you drank, and I have to confess I was jealous. I promise not to be such a fool in future. And I promise to share the driving when we go out.'

Brooke gaped her astonishment at these unexpected and amazing concessions. 'What in heaven's name did my mother say to you?'

'What should have been said years ago, but what I had already begun to work out for myself. I want you to be happily married to me, Brooke. I don't want to repress you, or control you. I thought I was protecting you, and our marriage, but I went about it the wrong way. Undoubtedly I learned some bad habits from my father, who's a bit old-fashioned in his ideas about marriage. Still, I honestly didn't realise you weren't content till this last week.'

Brooke sighed. 'Now that part's *my* fault, Leo. I should have stood up for myself earlier. I thought I was protecting our marriage too. So I just said yes to whatever you wanted, but sometimes I *wasn't* happy. I just pretended to be.'

'I did notice you pretending in bed, believe me. And I hated it. In future I want you to say no to whatever it is you don't want to do, sex included. Please...don't pretend. Ever.'

When tears suddenly threatened, Brooke steadfastly blinked them away. Tonight was not for tears. 'I...I'll do that in future, Leo. I guess I was afraid that if I was myself I might end up like...like...'

'Like your mother. Yes, I know. She told me all about that today. We had a good long chat, your mum and I. She straightened me out about something else as well.'

For a second Brooke feared her mother had spilled all her concerns about Francesca, about her going to Milan that day and seeing him at Francesca's apartment and jumping to the conclusion he was being unfaithful.

'Like...like what?' she choked out.

'Like the children's names. I rode roughshod over your feelings in that regard, Brooke, and I'm truly sorry. It was incredibly selfish and egotistical of me. But it's too late *now* to change their names, isn't it?'

'Yes, of course it is,' she agreed swiftly, touched by his ongoing concessions but a little agitated over the way this conversation was going. She wished she hadn't thought of Francesca. 'Still, your apology means the world to me, Leo. You've no idea. But let's not get too serious—or sorry—tonight. Tonight is for celebrating only. Why don't you open the first of those lovely bottles of champagne and we'll toast our future happiness?'

He seemed relieved to stop apologising as well.

'You're a wonderful woman, Brooke,' he said as he popped the cork and poured some of the fizzing liquid into the two crystal flutes provided, pressing one into her hand before taking the second for himself. 'To us!' he said, smiling.

'To us,' she echoed. Clinking the glasses, they both drank deeply.

'Another,' he insisted, refilling her glass.

For the next half-hour they devoured the delicious food and drank the truly divine champagne, going through the first bottle in no time and starting on the second. They put on some romantic music and settled themselves comfortably on the deep, squashy sofa with the food at the ready. Between succulent mouthfuls Leo would lean over and kiss her, long, deep, drugging kisses which sent her head spinning. Or was that the champagne already working?

Whatever, Brooke felt more light-hearted—and possibly light-headed—than she had in a long time. And incredibly sexy. She could not wait for Leo to stop eating and start making proper love to her.

They'd disposed of the main course and were down to the last few strawberries when Leo stood up. 'I think now is the perfect time for your present,' he announced.

'Oh, goodness! I'd forgotten all about that.'

'Shame on you,' he mocked. 'Now, you are to go over and stand at that big window right there. Face it and close your eyes.'

Brooke gulped, but she did as she was told.

Tension built in her as she stood there with her eyes tightly shut, trying not to think of the last time she'd stood in that same spot.

She couldn't hear anything except the music. The carpet was very thick and plush and the room was sound-proof. What was Leo doing? What could her present be?

When she suddenly felt his breath on the back of her neck, she stopped breathing; when something cold and metallic slipped round her throat, she gasped.

Her eyes flew open.

'Oh, Leo!' she cried.

The tinted glass in the window provided an excellent reflection and her hands came up to feel what she could already see: a necklace of exquisite delicacy and beauty, the setting like spun gold, into which were set five magnificent ruby-red stones from which fell five more ruby teardrops.

'They're not real, are they?' she said, twisting her head slightly to glance over her shoulder up at him.

His hand cupped her chin and he dropped a tender

kiss on her mouth. 'I told you, Brooke. There's nothing fake about tonight. And that includes this gift. It's as real as my love for you.'

Brooke's head whipped back to stare at it again in the window. 'But, Leo, it must have cost a fortune!'

'It did. Now, don't have a pink fit. I didn't buy it. It's a family treasure. An heirloom. Inherited from my grandmother, as well, to be given to my wife. Frankly, I'd forgotten about its existence till my mother reminded me. I thought it was just the thing to give you this anniversary. I knew it would go wonderfully with that dress, which is why I asked you to wear it.

'And I was right,' he said, curving his hands over her shoulders. 'It looks incredible. *You* look incredible.' His head dropped to her throat, his mouth hungry on her flesh, his voice low and thick. 'God, Brooke… It's been agony keeping my hands off you this long. I keep thinking of what's not under that dress and how much I want to touch you there.'

When his hands slid down her arms and onto her thighs Brooke moaned softly. When they started sliding back upwards, taking her dress with them, she could only stand and stare at the erotic image she made in the window as more and more of her legs were exposed. She could see Leo staring at them as well, his eyelids more hooded than usual. She could hear his heavy breathing in her ear.

Her head began to spin when the dress reached the top of her thighs. He hesitated at that point, then kept going, inch by breathless inch, till she was standing there, naked to the waist.

For several excruciatingly long seconds Leo kept her

that way, whilst he just stared at her. Her heart began hammering against her ribs, a wave of heat flushing the entire surface of her skin.

When his lips moved against her ear, she quivered uncontrollably.

'You look magnificent,' he murmured. 'But I think such a sight requires a lot closer attention…and far less clothing,' he added, smoothing the red velvet back down over her hips once more before lifting his hands to the zipper at the back of her neck.

Brooke gasped as the tightness of the dress abruptly gave way and a rush of cool air invaded her naked back. She watched, her head whirling, as Leo pushed the dress off her shoulders then dragged it downwards, till it peeled off her hands and hips, then dropped, like stone, to the carpet, leaving her standing there, wearing nothing but the ruby necklace, sheer skin-coloured stockings and five-inch gold sandals.

'Incredible,' Leo breathed, his eyes feasting on her image in the window. 'Irresistible.' Abruptly he scooped an arm under her jelly-like knees, lifted her up in his arms and carried her towards the bedroom.

Brooke might not have noticed the room and its contents at all if Leo hadn't stopped to switch on the light. She blinked first at the stark white walls, before dropping her gaze to the plush grey carpet, then finally focusing on the bed.

It was new and huge, with a black wrought-iron bedhead and a shimmering silver spread made of quilted satin.

Leo strode over and spread her heated body across its cool, silky smooth surface, trailing his hands down over her breasts and stomach before stroking her legs apart, then pulling her feet forwards till the heels of her shoes dangled over the edge.

Brooke held her breath the entire time.

'Now, don't move,' he commanded, turning away to walk back and close the door, then switch off the overhead light, plunging the room into darkness.

Immediately Brooke let out a shuddering sigh of relief.

But Leo didn't leave it at that. He drew back the black silk curtains to reveal the lights of the city, then returned to snap on the nearest of the ornate silver-based lamps which graced the glass bedside tables. The black silk shade threw a seductive glow over her entire body, spotlighting it for Leo's gaze, leaving absolutely nothing to the imagination.

Brooke felt both wildly excited and flushingly embarrassed. She wanted to close her legs, yet at the same time ached to open them even wider.

She did neither. She lay motionless, as ordered, watching wide-eyed, heart now thundering, while Leo undressed. He didn't hurry, taking his time to drape his clothes carefully over a chair in the corner. He even set his shoes and socks neatly underneath. But his eyes never strayed far from her body—or for long—yet, oddly, they seemed calm and cool.

At long last he was naked, and Brooke could see he was not nearly as calm—or cool—as he was making out. Far from it. Her own state of arousal was a revelation as well. Already she was on the brink. And he hadn't even touched her. She'd never felt the like in her life. She wanted him. Now! This very second!

Disobediently, her legs dared to part a little further, and she thrilled to the sudden wild flaring in his eyes.

But he made no move to join her, just stood there beside the bed, staring down at her.

'Oh, please, Leo,' she moaned. 'Please...'

'Patience, tiger woman,' he drawled. 'You must learn that the pleasure is more in the chase than the kill.'

She could not believe it when he sat down between her legs, his back to her, and slowly, ever so slowly, removed her shoes and then her stockings. She had never known such an agony of frustration as his fingers feathered over her ankles and toes, her calves, her knees, her thighs. He touched her everywhere but where she wanted him to touch.

She was at screaming point when he finally turned round to face her.

It was then that the real torture began.

'Oh, no, Leo, no,' she choked out when he began touching her where she'd been dying to be touched. Because by then she was wanting something else. She was wanting him, inside her, filling her, loving her.

But he ignored her protest and of course she came almost immediately, one of those electric little climaxes which race through you like lightning but leave you wanting more.

She protested again when he bent to give her more, with his mouth as well as his hands. She thought she could not possibly come again so soon.

But she did.

'Oh, Leo,' she gasped. 'Leo...'

'Yes, my love?' he murmured as he moved over and

into her at last, taking her breath away with the power of his penetration.

But surely it was too late for her to do anything but lie limply in his arms.

Once again, she was wrong.

With each surge of his flesh into hers she stirred a little, till she was clinging to him and moaning with renewed need.

'Yes…*yes*,' she cried out, her nails digging into his back as the exquisite tension built to crisis point in her once more.

'I can't hold on any longer, Brooke,' Leo groaned.

But then they were both there, together, and Brooke was crying out with delight.

Happiness, she decided afterwards, as she drifted slowly down from her rapture, was being made love to by Leo, her darling, wonderful, incredible Leo. The desperation of the previous week was totally forgotten. Her doubts and her fears all gone.

'I love you, Leo,' she whispered, when she could manage to speak.

'And I love you, Signora Parini,' he returned, holding her face while he poured kisses all over it. 'Only you. Only ever you.'

CHAPTER TEN

'THIS is the life,' Brooke murmured as she leant back in the spa bath.

Leo had let her cat-nap while he ran it, kissing her awake before carrying her into the bathroom where the lavish round tub was full to breast height with warm, scented water and the frothiest bubbles she'd ever seen.

Once she was deposited safely in one end, Leo had gone to collect the ice bucket with what was left of the champagne—just enough for one glass each. He'd poured them out, then joined her in the bath, and now they were both lying back, facing each other, enjoying the massaging effect of the water jets on their gentlest setting.

Brooke glanced idly around at the very opulent-looking bathroom as she sipped the last of the lovely bubbly. There hadn't been a spa bath in here five years ago, just the old-fashioned claw-footed variety, in keeping with the then country look. Everything had been cream and green back then, with a large wooden vanity and old-fashioned taps.

Now, all the walls, floors and benches were black marble, the kind which had grey and gilt veins running through it. The bath, basins and toilet were a pearly white, the trim and tap fittings gold, as were the exotic light fittings. The huge mirrored cabinet above the vanity was gilt-edged as well.

The effect was very rich and very decadent.

Brooke realised with a measure of surprise that she'd never had a bath with Leo before, not even before they were married. Showers, yes, but not a bath.

It was lovely. Relaxing, yet exciting at the same time. Only their toes were touching at the moment, and they couldn't see too much of each other's bodies. But the knowledge that they were both naked beneath the bubbles added a stimulating edge to the experience.

'I should do this more often,' Leo said.

'Do *what* more often?' she asked, her blue eyes dancing.

'Get the children minded for the night, then take you off somewhere private and romantic where I can make mad, passionate love to you all night.'

'Promises, promises. It's only ten o'clock, and you've only made love to me once so far.'

'Darling wife, I started making love to you the moment I rang this morning and ordered your underwear off. You've been turned on all day, Signora Parini. Why don't you just admit it?'

'What about *you*, Signor Parini?' she countered, refusing to admit a thing. 'Were *you* turned on all day, thinking about tonight?'

'I deliberately distracted myself with one project after another, as you might have noticed. But I still had to have the longest, coldest shower before I came to pick you up. I couldn't afford to disappoint you. Not tonight.'

She smiled softly. 'You never disappoint me, Leo.'

'Really? What about those times you faked things this last year?'

Brooke shrugged. 'I just wasn't in the mood. I don't know why. Tired, I guess. Valentino himself couldn't have aroused me on those nights.'

'I don't think I tried too hard,' Leo muttered. 'And I'm not so sure you were tired as much as discontented. I've been a selfish, self-centred husband, Brooke, and I'm so sorry. But things will be better from now on.'

Brooke was touched by his sincere apology and his promise to do better. If tonight was anything to go by, the future looked very rosy indeed.

'Now!' he said as he lowered his empty glass onto the marble floor then glanced up at her with a wicked gleam in his beautiful black eyes. 'Should I order another bottle of champagne before the next round begins?'

'Mmm. Not unless you're planning on making love to one very sleepy lady.'

'Heaven forbid! In that case, nothing but coffee for you from now on. I have no intention of letting you sleep yet, tiger woman. The night is still young, and you look incredibly desirable sitting there in the water, with your hair slightly tousled, your shoulders bare and that ruby necklace around your deliciously inviting throat.'

'Goodness!' she said, only just remembering it was still there. Hurriedly she put down her near empty glass too, sat up straight and lifted her hands to the clasp at the back of her neck.

'No, don't take it off,' Leo protested. 'It looks gorgeous. Besides, it's made of real gold and real rubies. A bit of soap and water won't ruin it.'

'Really? Are you sure? Oh…all right, then. I suppose you're right.' She touched it reverently with her fingertips. 'I've never owned anything so beautiful before, or so expensive. I just love it, Leo. It was the perfect anniversary present.'

'Yes, I thought so too,' he agreed, his eyes warm and loving. 'Giving it to you tonight worked out very well.'

She was leaning back again when a niggling thought struck. Leo was not the sort of man to forget anything. His memory was second to none. So *why* hadn't he given her the necklace before? Could the delay have something to do with Francesca?

Her stomach curled at this unpleasant idea.

'Leo...' she said, possessed by a sudden determination to find out some more answers about his relationship with Francesca. Such as when *had* he finally got over his infatuation for her? And what did he think of the woman now that Lorenzo was dead? Did he hate her still? Or pity her?

Brooke would also have liked to ask him what, exactly, he had been doing in her apartment that day. But she didn't dare. That would mean admitting she'd been there, which would lead to Leo's asking her why. Then she'd have to explain that his mother had said a good deal more than Brooke had confessed to overhearing.

'Yes, what's the problem?' Leo probed.

Brooke swallowed. 'You...you said there were to be no more secrets between us.'

'Ye...es?' He looked and sounded very wary all of a sudden.

Brooke's courage immediately failed her. Why spoil this wonderful night? she reasoned swiftly, trying to find excuses for her sudden lack of resolve. What more did she want from this man, damn it? He'd said he loved her, only her, always her. What more could he say to reassure her?

'Brooke? What do you want to say?' Leo insisted. 'Come on…you can't hold back now.'

Brooke could, and she would. All she had to do was think of something else to ask instead.

'Why didn't you ever ask me about the boyfriends I had before you?' she blurted out.

His eyebrows arched, then he laughed. 'I opted for blissful ignorance on that score. Besides, I wasn't sure if there was enough time in the world to hear about them *all*.'

'Oh! Oh, you…' She whooshed across to his side of the bath, kneeling on either side of his legs and leaning forward to pummel him playfully on his shoulders and chest. 'You know I didn't have all that many! And you know none of them meant a thing…once I met you.'

'Good,' he growled, grabbing her upper arms and hauling her right up onto him, her soap-slicked nipples grazing over the wet curls which covered his chest. At the same time her stomach rode up over what felt like a very formidable erection indeed.

'Oh, you beast!' she cried out when his grip tightened and he rubbed her up and down against it.

His smile was almost a grimace. 'Lady, you don't know the half of it.'

'Are you telling me that's only *half* of it?' she taunted, doing a little rubbing herself. Heat had instantly licked along her veins at the feel of him, excitement and desire mixing to make her bold.

'Don't tease me, Brooke,' Leo said thickly.

'Who's teasing?' she breathed, and reached down to take him in her hand and insert him deep into her body.

When he groaned, she stretched up to cover his lips with her own, sending her tongue briefly into his startled mouth before retreating and sitting back up straight. He groaned again, and a wave of the most intoxicating triumph washed through her.

She found herself smiling down at him. Who was in control *now*? It was *his* turn to squirm, to be taken to the edge and over, while *she* watched *him*.

'Let's see who can last the longest *this* time,' she challenged, and reached up to take the pins from her hair, shaking her long blonde hair out over her shoulders.

Leo's dark eyes narrowed upon her. Then *he* smiled. 'Loser makes the coffee?' he suggested silkily.

Brooke tried not to look too smug. If Leo thought he had the upper hand this time, then he was in for a surprise. She was on top. *She* would control the action.

Besides, she'd already had three orgasms to his one, Brooke thought with wicked glee. No way would she be coming quickly *this* time!

Slowly, voluptuously, she began to rise and fall upon him, her hard-tipped breasts becoming more and more visible as the soapy bubbles dripped off them. She watched his lips pull back from his teeth as he sucked in sharply; watched his eyes close and his nostrils flare; watched the body language of a man being carried swiftly to the point of no return.

Oh, yes. This time *she* was going to win.

*   *   *

'You look positively wrecked,' were her mother's first words the next day, once Leo had left and the children's maniacal greetings had died down. They had finally been persuaded out into the back yard to play, at which point Brooke sank down on a kitchen stool with a weary sigh.

'Can I get you a cup of coffee?' her mother offered.

Brooke groaned. 'Lord, no. No more coffee. I'm already suffering from caffeine overload.'

'Then how was last night? Or dare I ask? Leo certainly seemed happy enough this morning.'

'That man! Doesn't he ever need sleep? And can't he ever *bear* to lose a bet?'

Phyllis gave her daughter a droll look. 'I take it last night went well, then? For Leo, anyway.'

'For me, too. I won't be a hypocrite and say I didn't enjoy myself. I'm just exhausted.'

'Would that *I* could feel exhausted some morning for the same reason!' Phyllis exclaimed.

Brooke had to laugh. 'Were the children any trouble?'

'Not a bit.'

'You're sure?'

'Positive. As good as gold. Now, are you still up to some shopping this morning? Say so if you're not.'

'Why not? As tired as I am, I haven't a hope of actually sleeping till some of this caffeine wears off. I might get a nap when we get back and the kids go to bed.'

Brooke struggled through the next couple of hours, but it was worth it to see the happiness on her mother's face. She steered her mother into the right kind of dress shop, which had just the thing for the more mature career woman who wanted to look up to date and attractive without crossing the line into mutton dressed up as lamb.

Phyllis splurged out on three three-piece suits which Brooke showed her could carry her through from day to night, depending on what accessories were worn with them. One was red, one black and one cream. Brooke suggested black accessories for all three, conservative pumps and a roomy handbag for daywear, strappy high heels and a clutch purse for after five. She also showed her mother how to mix and match the outfits, and how, by adding a camisole or a scarf, or a little knitted top, or even the right jewellery, she could create an entirely different look.

'You're so knowledgeable about fashion,' her mother complimented her after they'd arrived home and were sitting over a sandwich. 'No wonder Leo wants you to go in with him on this business venture. I think you'll be brilliant! But then I'm biased, I guess. You're my daughter. But I always *did* think you were brilliant. That's why I got mad at your wasting yourself as a glorified clerk.'

'Mum, your intellectual snobbery is showing. Serving the public is a very skilled and demanding job, if you do it properly. Alessandro! For pity's sake, stop teasing poor Mister Puss and go back outside and play. Take Claudia with you.'

'But I don't want to,' he grumbled.

'Do as I say,' she pronounced firmly. 'Or you will go to your room and stay there till your father comes home!'

Her son's eyes widened at this threat of such a long term of punishment. Brooke could see his mind ticking over and wondering if she meant it.

Apparently, he decided, she did.

'Come on, Claudia,' he muttered, taking his sister's hand. 'Mummy's in a bad mood.' He sighed like a little old man and Brooke shook her head.

'Sometimes I think that boy's four going on eighty.'

'He's a darling. But he's going to be a handful when he grows up. You're going to have girls wall-to-wall and running after him.'

'Tell me about it. I have the same problem with his father. You should have seen this redhead behind the desk last night at the hotel, batting her eyelashes at him.'

'Like you once did, you mean?' Phyllis teased.

'Yes…well…that was different.'

'How?'

'He wasn't a married man then. Single girls have no respect for married men these days. Which reminds me, Mum. Your…er…potential boyfriend…'

'Matthew?'

'Yes, Matthew. He's not married, is he?'

'No. Divorced. Like me.'

'How many times?'

'I haven't asked.'

'I think you should.'

'No, Brooke, I'm not going to. I'm going to take him as he is. And hopefully he'll do the same with me.'

'But, Mum, sometimes the past is important.'

'You mean like Leo and Francesca? Goodness, girl, don't tell me you're still worrying about *that*!'

'I…well…yes, I am a little.'

'Then stop it. Right now! Leo loves you. You should have heard him on the phone to me yesterday, wanting to know what else he could do to make you happy. No way would that man look sidewards at another woman.'

Brooke scooped in a deep, gathering breath, then let it out slowly. 'I suppose you're right.'

'I know I am.'

'You've certainly changed your tune.'

'It's a woman's privilege to change her mind, isn't it?'

'Maybe, but when you change yours, you certainly go the whole hog! Next thing you'll be getting married again.'

'Now that's going too far. Some nice companionship and some great sex I could do with. But marriage? No way. Not for me. I'm not that much of a fool.'

'Like me, you mean?'

'Not at all. But I have to be honest, Brooke, men like Leo don't come along every day of the week.'

Brooke wasn't sure if she liked her mother complimenting Leo so much. He wasn't *perfect*. Not by any means. She was almost glad to see him looking the worse for wear by the time he arrived home that night. It was just too irritating for words being married to a superman.

'I take it we shall be having an early night tonight?' she said cheekily over dinner.

His instant alarm amused her. 'No, Leo, that's not

what I meant. I just meant you look as wrecked as my mother said *I* looked all day.'

Leo groaned. 'I don't know how I functioned today. I had to go and see Vince again, like I promised, but I was brain dead as well as body dead. In the end we agreed to meet again this weekend. I invited him over on Saturday. Is that all right with you?'

'Perfectly all right,' she agreed happily. The Leo of last week would not have asked her that. He would have just announced the fact that Vince was coming. Maybe he *was* perfect, after all!

Brooke went to bed that night with good thoughts. Her mother was right. She was silly to keep worrying about Francesca. Leo loved *her*. Francesca was the past, not the present...

CHAPTER ELEVEN

MONDAY was playgroup morning, when Brooke took the children down to a local hall where she mixed with other mothers of pre-school children whilst the children played with each other. Alessandro just loved the company of other boys his age, and expended a lot of energy on these mornings playing chasings, whilst Claudia tended to sit quietly with one or two of the little girls and dress up dollies.

Normally Brooke joined into conversation with the other mothers on these occasions, but on that Monday she found herself often falling silent, her mind going back over the weekend just past.

Vince had come on the Saturday afternoon, arriving around two and not leaving till late that night. Brooke had liked him enormously from the moment he walked in the door. Shortish and quite thin, he was still very good-looking, with spiky blond hair and wicked blue eyes. Obviously gay, he had a charm and a wit which was both engaging and entertaining, and he had made Brooke laugh with his saucy tales of the model and fashion world. He'd been good with the children too, reading them stories while Brooke cooked the dinner.

It hadn't been till the following day that Brooke had realised how much Leo had taken a back seat the day before and let Vince and herself do most of the talking.

She'd been touched by his generosity, and had told him so as soon as he woke up on the Sunday morning.

'No need to thank me,' he told her, yawning and stretching. 'I enjoyed watching the interplay between you two. You and Vince are going to make a great team. I can see my investment will be in safe hands. Besides,' he added, smiling, 'with Vince being gay, I have no worries on *that* little score.'

Brooke frowned at that remark. 'Would you ever really worry about me on that score, Leo? What if Vince hadn't been gay?'

'Then I wouldn't have let him within a million miles of you,' he replied in all seriousness.

'But why? Don't you trust me?'

'I trust *you*. I simply don't trust men.'

'But *you're* a man,' she pointed out.

'Exactly.' He grinned and pulled her to him. 'You wouldn't have been safe with me for a minute, even if you'd been married to another man. I had to have you the moment I saw you.'

'Leo, you're not serious!'

'I certainly am. Very serious. Now, do shut up and kiss me. It's Sunday morning and I don't have to go to work.'

'Ah, yes, but *I* do,' she said, and, throwing back the covers, Brooke scuttled out of the bed to see why Claudia was crying.

Now, Brooke kept mulling over Leo's words. Had he meant what he'd said? Would he have seduced her even if she *had* been married? Was he that kind of man? Ruthless? Predatory? *Conscienceless?*

She didn't like that thought, not one little bit.

It plagued her mind from that moment on, so much so that by the time she arrived home, around noon, she was unable to eat, or even open the mail. They were all bills, anyway.

She fed the children and put them to bed for their nap, then sat and idly watched one of the soaps on TV. Not the best thing to watch in her present frame of mind. The characters led such tortured and tangled lives, full of affairs and intrigues, arguments and break-ups. Brooke had always craved a peaceful life, emotionally. She could not bear confrontation or argument.

Eventually she switched off the television, and was about to do some ironing when she heard the phone's soft ring. She always turned the sound down during the children's sleep, and hurried along to the extension in her bedroom to answer it.

'Yes?' She sat down on the edge of the bed.

'Brooke. Leo, here. Look, something awful's happened at home and I have to fly back straight away.'

Brooke immediately thought of Leo's father, with his heart problems. 'Is it your father? Has he had a heart attack?'

'No. Thank God. When I said home, I meant Italy, not Lake Como. It's Francesca. She's tried to kill herself. Took an overdose of sleeping tablets.'

Brooke's head spun. 'But...but *why*?' she blurted out. 'I mean...'

Leo sighed. 'I guess, in the end, she wasn't able to cope. Frankly, I was worried something like this might happen. Would you pack a small case for me, Brooke? Just enough for a couple of days. I've managed to get a seat on the afternoon flight to Rome, then a connecting flight to Milan in the morning.'

Brooke tried to keep calm, but inside all hell was breaking loose. 'But, Leo, why do *you* have to go? What about Francesca's family?'

'She doesn't have any.'

'Then what about your mother and father? Can't they help? They're only an hour away.'

'They can't know anything about this, Brooke. It would probably kill my father.'

'But *why*? I can understand why a grieving widow might attempt suicide, especially when she doesn't have any children. I don't think your parents would be too shocked, Leo.'

'Trust me on this, Brooke. They would be if they knew all the facts. And I can't trust Francesca not to tell them. Unfortunately, I'm the only one who can help Francesca at this point in time. It's a damned nuisance, but that's just the way it is.'

'Tell them what? What are you talking about, Leo?'

'I can't explain everything now, Brooke. There simply isn't time. Pack a bag for me, like a good girl. I'll be by in ten minutes to pick it up.'

He hung up. He actually hung up. Brooke just stared into the dead phone. Her husband was dropping everything and flying off to the other side of the world to be by the side of a woman he supposedly no longer loved!

It was incredible!

Unbelievable!

Unbearable!

Brooke packed the bag in a daze, all the while desperately trying to think of something to say to stop him going.

She was standing at the front gate with the bag at her feet when he drove up and jumped out of his car.

'Sorry about this,' he said, bending to kiss her cheek and pick up the bag at the same time. 'I'll be back by Friday. I've rung everyone I needed to, explaining I've been unexpectedly called away for a few days. If my mother or father ring, make up some excuse for why I'm not there. Tell them I'm talking business with Vince. Tell them anything. They're not to know the truth, Brooke. That's imperative. Promise me.'

'I...I promise.'

'Good girl. Now, don't look so worried. I'll explain everything when I get back. No time right now. I'm only just going to make the plane as it is.'

She followed him over to the car. 'You...you will ring me when you get there, won't you, Leo?'

'What?' he said distractedly as he tossed the bag into the passenger seat and climbed in behind the wheel. 'Oh, yes...yes, of course I will.'

'You can explain everything then,' she pointed out tautly, and he gave her a sharp look.

'You're not still worried about me and Francesca, are you? Yes, I can see you are, but you don't have to be, darling. She'd be the last woman on earth I'd touch. I'm really sorry but I must go or I'll miss the plane. Love you!' He slammed the car door shut and wound down the window. 'I'll ring as soon as I can and tell you the whole long wretched story.'

She watched him roar off, her heart sinking. She wanted to trust him. She really did. He'd sounded so sincere. And he'd said he loved her. He'd been saying that a lot lately.

If only he'd had time to explain *now*.

Regret that she hadn't tackled her husband more forcibly about his relationship with Francesca tormented Brooke all afternoon. She should not have been so weak. She should have asked him for details over their engagement and break-up.

It was well after tea before Brooke finally got round to opening the bills which had arrived that morning. The first was the telephone bill for their home line, and the amount startled Brooke. It was higher than she would have expected, considering they'd spent three weeks away in Italy during the last quarter.

Automatically, she scanned down the list of calls, stopping when she came across two overseas calls on the one day, one far more expensive than the other. The first was to Leo's parents, made on the Sunday they returned. Sixteen minutes.

The second was to a Milan number—one Brooke wasn't familiar with—and it had lasted nearly two hours! The time recorded stated the call had begun at five past two that same Sunday and finished right on four, around the time she'd arrived home from her mother's.

Brooke stared at the number, her heart racing. She knew it wasn't the office in Milan. She knew that number off by heart.

Dread filled her soul as she walked over to the drawer where they kept their telephone and address book. Pulling it out, she flicked open the book to the 'P's, her heart lurching once she saw the number attached to Lorenzo Parini's Milan address. It was one and the same as the number on the bill. Leo had rung Francesca whilst *she'd* been out of the house and talked to the woman for two *hours*!

Brooke burst into tears. How could he? The traitor. The liar. The...the...*bastard*!

Sobbing furiously, she ripped open the second bill, addressed personally to Leo. Again it was a telephone bill, that of his mobile phone, the one he took with him everywhere.

With eyes blurred and shoulders shaking, Brooke searched for the same number amongst the pages. And there it was, not once but three times. Okay, so they weren't long calls, usually only a few minutes, but one really pained her. Because it had taken place on Wednesday night, at eight minutes past seven, the time when Leo would have been getting ready for their anniversary night together.

Yet he'd stopped to ring Francesca. What did that tell her, his wife?

That her husband was a lying, conniving, adulterous bastard, that he'd seduced Francesca at long last—either out of ego or revenge—and was conducting a long-distance affair whilst he soothed his silly wife's suspicion with exactly the same tools he'd probably used with Francesca. Lies and sex.

She didn't believe Francesca had tried to kill herself for a moment. Not seriously. She wasn't dead, *was* she? It was nothing more than a ploy to get Leo to fly back to her and give her some more of what she was now missing. Leo, in her bed. Leo, telling her he *had* to go back to his wife, for his children's sake, but it was *her* he really loved. Her. Always her.

Just as Leo's mother had said.

Brooke went from dismay to distress to despair, then finally to destruction. Not her own. Leo's!

She would not turn a blind eye this time. She would not remain quietly in the background, like a good little girl. She would not roll over and put her legs in the air, like a dead cockroach. Or like the stupid whore she'd been last Wednesday night!

Clenching her teeth hard in her jaw, Brooke looked up their travel agent's number in the book and dialled. She couldn't get a seat on tomorrow's direct flight to Rome, but she could fly with another airline's morning flight to Zurich, followed by a fairly quick connection to Milan. With no unforeseen delays, she would arrive at Francesca's apartment less than a day after Leo.

Provided, of course, she could get her mother to mind the children. It would be a big ask, but this was a real emergency.

'Of course I'll mind the children,' her mother offered as soon as Brooke had poured out the whole story. 'I'll take the rest of the week off. But don't go to the trouble of bringing them over here. I'll come over and stay in your house. Children are best in their own environment if it's going to be for more than a day or two.'

'Oh, Mum, thank you, thank you. I'll never be able to repay you.'

'Nonsense. What are mothers for? Now, don't you worry about a thing at this end, Brooke. Lord knows what's going on between Leo and that woman, but I agree you can't sit back this time and do nothing.

Though I still don't believe Leo's been unfaithful to you. The more I think about it, I think he's being manipulated by a very devious and quite evil woman. She dropped Leo in favour of Lorenzo when it suited her—no doubt because he was the older son and possibly the richer brother—and now that he's dead she's switched her attentions back to Leo.'

Brooke was truly taken aback. She'd never thought of Francesca in that light before. The woman had always seemed such a weak, wishy-washy creature, with no get up and go!

But maybe her mother was right. Maybe, underneath, Francesca played at being fragile to bring out the protective instinct of men, to draw them into her web, so to speak.

Then, once they were there, she kept them captive with the sort of sex men could not resist. Brooke had no doubt Francesca was good in bed. There was an unconscious air of sensuality about the woman which she couldn't hide.

Brooke clutched onto the hope that she'd been directing her anger at the wrong person. Maybe it wasn't Leo she should want to destroy, but Francesca!

But then she remembered the phone calls, and *both* of them lay condemned in her eyes.

'Maybe you're right, Mum,' she said coldly. 'But I wouldn't put my house on it if I were you. Oh, and Mum, when Leo rings tomorrow morning—and he will—don't tell him that I'm on my way there. Tell him I'm sick and that's why you've answered the phone. Tell him I'm in bed asleep and suggest he rings back later in the day. By then I'll be there, and the bastard will wish I wasn't!'

'Oh, Brooke, I hate to hear you sound so hard.'

'There are times in life, Mum, when only hard will do. Now I have to pack and sort out my clothes. See you later.'

CHAPTER TWELVE

BROOKE looked down at her black suit and wondered if, subconsciously, she'd dressed for grieving.

The anger which had carried her onto the plane bound for Zurich had long dissipated by the time she'd arrived, and it had been a very dispirited Brooke who had boarded the connecting flight for Milan. By the time *that* arrived, she'd been close to breaking down, the awful reality of her situation sinking in.

Her husband didn't really love her.

He had deceived her.

Her marriage was probably over.

Once in the taxi on her way to Francesca's apartment, however, Brooke experienced some resurgence of spirit. If she was going to lose her husband to another woman then she would go down fighting. Pride demanded it.

So did the slim hope that her mother *might* be right, and Francesca was the real culprit.

Brooke felt almost flattered when the doorman recognised her and let her into the building without a quibble, and without ringing Francesca's apartment to check if she was expected. Brooke didn't want the illicit lovers to have any time to dress, or arrange the apartment, or even make the bed!

Francesca had never hired live-in servants, despite Lorenzo having been extremely wealthy. She had once confessed to Brooke that she didn't like the feeling of people spying on her, so she hired cleaners and cooks and maids to come in when required. They never slept over.

'My husband is in, is he?' Brooke asked the doorman sweetly in Italian.

She was told that, yes, Signor Parini was definitely in. He hadn't left the apartment since he'd arrived the previous day.

Brooke's stomach churned some more at this news. But she was determined to see things through this time. No more running away.

'Shall I carry your case up for you, Signora Parini?' the doorman offered.

Politely, she declined the offer. She only had a small bag. She wasn't planning on staying long.

Her stomach was in knots by the time she stood outside the solid apartment door on the first floor, her hands on the doorbell. When a perfectly strange woman answered, Brooke was truly startled.

About forty, she was tall and large, with a kind face and an impressive bosom.

Introducing herself in Italian, Brooke quickly found out the woman was a nurse, hired by Leo to help mind Francesca after the 'accident'.

Brooke absorbed this information warily.

So Francesca *had* tried to kill herself. And Leo *had* been of help. That still didn't make either of them innocent.

'Where is my husband now?' Brooke enquired, putting on an innocent expression.

He was upstairs, she was told, sitting with Francesca

in her room. Did the *signora* want her to go up and let
Signor Parini know his wife was here?

'No, no,' Brooke said swiftly. 'I'm expected. And I
know the way. How *is* Francesca this morning?'

'Much better.'

I'll just bet she is, Brooke thought, all her earlier
fury flooding back.

Francesca's apartment was huge, occupying half of
two floors. The floors and stairs were all Italian marble,
with lots of mirrors and decorative columns everywhere. Brooke had always thought it a showy, gaudy,
decadent-looking place, just like Lorenzo.

Francesca's bedroom was to the immediate left of
the upstairs landing, and Brooke's heart was squeezing
tighter and tighter as she mounted each step. Dread of
what she would find behind its door gripped her chest,
and her soul.

The door, however, wasn't closed, and from the moment she reached the landing Brooke could see into the
room. From where she was standing, all she could see
was the foot of the four-poster bed, but if she moved
closer and around to the left she might be able to see
more. And *hear* more.

A low, muffled voice was drifting through the doorway. A woman's voice. Francesca was talking, saying
things that Brooke wanted to hear, *had* to hear.

She tiptoed closer and to the left, into a position
where she could see half of Leo. He was sitting in a
chair on the other side of the bed, leaning forward, his
body language that of an intense and caring listener.
She could not see his face, just a side view of the back
of his dark head.

Francesca's face was also out of view, but by the position of her feet under the covers she was lying down in the bed, well over to the side Leo was sitting on. Brooke pictured her lying there all pale and wan, a tragic beauty, her wavy shoulder-length black hair spread out on snow-white pillows.

Brooke inched as close as she dared, finding a spot where she could not be seen but from where *she* could see a good deal, plus hear every word.

'You…didn't…*couldn't*…understand,' Francesca was saying in an emotion-charged voice. 'And how could I explain it? But I did love you, Leonardo. You were the only man who'd ever been like that with me. So kind. And caring. So considerate, even when I kept you at arm's length. But I was afraid to sleep with you back then. Afraid you would find out I was not the sweet, innocent virgin you thought me to be. And then Lorenzo turned up, and he…well, you know now what happened with Lorenzo.'

'Yes,' Leo said, sighing. 'I know *now*, Francesca. But I didn't know any of this at the time. How do you think I felt when I came into my brother's bedroom and saw what I saw?'

'Oh, Leonardo,' she cried piteously. 'Don't remind me. It was wicked of us, I know. But then I *am* wicked. I must be, to do the things that I've done. And I'm still doing them. I feel so guilty and so ashamed. Barely two weeks after Lorenzo died and I'm in bed with…' A sob choked off her words.

'Now, now,' Leo soothed. 'Don't upset yourself again. What's done is done. And it was inevitable, Francesca. It wasn't really your fault.'

'You keep saying that, Leonardo, but I can't keep blaming the men in my life. It must be something in *me* which brings out the worst in them. You're the only one who's ever treated me decently. Oh, God…why didn't I marry you when I had the chance?'

Brooke had heard enough. She stepped forward just in time to see Francesca reach out to place a tender hand against Leo's cheek. He was actually covering it with his own and looking sadly down at her when Brooke moved into the doorway and just stood there, watching and waiting for their guilt to manifest itself.

Francesca gasped, and snatched her hand away.

Leo's eyes did snap up and around, but he looked more astounded than guilty. 'Brooke!' he exclaimed, and rose swiftly to his feet. 'What on earth are you doing *here*? Your mother said that…'

'My mother lied to you,' she broke in, in Italian, so Francesca could understand exactly what she was saying. 'I followed you here so that I could catch you and this…*slut*…in the act.'

She actually used the Italian, *puttana*, which encompassed rather more than 'slut'. It was the worst word she could think of.

'I didn't quite manage that,' she went on bitterly, 'but I saw and heard enough just now to know the score.'

'Brooke, you've got it all wrong,' Leo insisted, panic on his handsome face.

'Oh, please…don't take me for a fool any more.' Her voice was hard and cold and scathing in its contempt. But inside her heart was crumbling to nothing. 'To be brutally frank, I already had my suspicions.

Remember the day of my headache? I didn't go to bed that afternoon. I drove in here and sat outside this apartment, being sick in the gutter at what I saw. *Your* car in the car park, Leo. My husband, not working hard at the office, but here, in bed with his sweet sister-in-law.'

Francesca groaned and buried her face in the pillow, while Leo gaped at her. 'What, in God's name, possessed you to even *think* such a thing?'

Brooke's returning look was scornful. He'd stopped denying everything, she noticed.

'Actually, I'd overheard your mother saying a good bit more than I told you, Leo. She expressed concern you were still in love with your old fiancée and that you might not be working late at the office every night. She was afraid you might be here, with Francesca, enjoying what you apparently never enjoyed when you were engaged.'

By this time Leo was ashen, whilst Francesca was shaking her head and sobbing into her hands.

'Lord knows how *that* happened,' Brooke scorned. 'Given you're such a stud and she's the slut of all time. But I could see if that was the case then she would have held some kind of lasting fascination for you. I told myself it was a one-off, that you didn't really love her, it was only an ego or a revenge thing. So, brave little wife and blind, lovesick fool that I was, I determined to get you back, so I...I...'

Brooke's voice broke as emotion threatened to engulf her.

'And *you*,' she threw at Leo as she struggled to fight back tears. 'You let me. You let me humiliate myself in ways which I shudder to think about now. Everyone told me to turn a blind eye, even my own mother. So I did. But I just couldn't do it any longer, not once I found out about the phone calls.'

'The phone calls?' Leo repeated blankly.

'Yes, goddamn it, the phone calls! To this... *creature*! The phone bills came in the day you dropped everything and flew off here. There was one to this number on our account for two bloody hours! So I opened the bill for your mobile and there were more, with one even on the night of our anniversary!'

Leo groaned. 'Brooke, for pity's sake, let me explain!'

'You can't, Leo. It's gone past explaining. I won't believe you, no matter what you say. I want a divorce. And I want the children.'

His chin shot up, determination stamped all over his arrogantly handsome face. 'Well, you can't have them! And you can't have a divorce, either.'

'Can't I just? We'll see about that!' she spat. 'If you recall, my mother is a lawyer, and a damned good one. She'll get my children for me. They won't be allowed anywhere near you and your filthy whore!'

Not once in all the time she'd known Leo had she seen him so shaken. For a split second he just stood there, staring at her.

But then he rallied, his voice strong and reasoned, his eyes intense on hers. 'Brooke, you *have* to listen,' he began. 'For our children's sake, if not for mine. This is not what you think. You've got it all wrong. I love *you*, not Francesca. I've *never* slept with her. All I've been doing is talk to her, try to help her after Lorenzo's death.'

'You expect me to believe that? Then who was it Francesca slept with so soon after her darling husband's death? Who is it who's driven her to *this*!' And she waved a contemptuous hand at the wretched figure weeping in the bed. 'Oh, no, Leo, no…you're quite wrong. I don't *have* to listen to any more lies. I'm out of here. You both make me sick to my stomach.'

She whirled away to leave, but Leo was across the room before she'd taken two strides, grabbing her left arm and whirling her back to face him. Driven to breaking point, Brooke lashed out with her free arm, her hand cracking him across the face with an open palm. He gasped with shock, and so did she, once she saw the ugly red imprint of her blow flare up on his cheek.

'Stop it—stop it!' Francesca screamed as she sat bolt upright in the bed with wild eyes and even wilder hair. 'It wasn't Leonardo I slept with, Brooke. It was a perfect stranger, some man I'd picked up at a bar. I brought him home here and I…I let him do things to me in my husband's bed that nice girls like you don't even *know* about!'

Brooke gaped while Leo groaned. 'Francesca, you don't have to do this. Brooke will understand once I explain everything to her…in *private*.'

'No, no, Leonardo, she has to know it all,' Francesca cried. 'From *me*. And then she'll believe you. I can't bear for you to suffer because of me. Not you. You're the only good man I've ever known.

'But there are bad men out there, Brooke,' she raved

on, madness in her eyes. 'Really bad men. My father was one of them.'

'Your…father?' Brooke echoed.

'Yes. My father. My darling, beloved father whom I adored. When my mother died, I was only twelve. The night she was buried he brought me into his bed to take her place. And the next night. And every night after that.'

Brooke sucked in sharply. She had heard of such things happening, but she'd never actually met someone it had happened to.

'Can you imagine a father doing that to his daughter?'

An appalled Brooke could only shake her head.

'By the time I was sixteen he had removed me permanently from school to play wife for him all the time. He was a rich man, you see. He didn't need to go to work if he didn't want to. So we travelled the world together, and he always introduced me as his daughter. But behind closed doors I wasn't his daughter. I was his whore, his very willing little whore.'

Brooke gasped, and Francesca smiled, a chilling little smile which made Brooke's blood run cold.

'That shocks you, doesn't it? That I would be willing by then. But just think…what else did I know? And we all want to be loved, even if that love is corrupt and evil, like my father's. My mother killed herself, you know, just to get away from him.'

'Francesca, that's enough!' Leo said firmly, but she would not be silenced.

'No, Leonardo! You keep advising me to tell a doctor, that talking about it might help. Well, I think telling your wife will help me more. Because she *needs* to know. Because then she'll believe you.'

'Let me at least close the door,' Leo muttered. 'There's no need for anyone else to hear this, surely.'

While he went to do so, a shaky Brooke settled herself on the side of the bed and told Francesca to continue. Leo just shook his head and went over to stare through the bedroom window. Clearly he'd heard the gruesome details before, and didn't want to hear them all again.

Francesca pushed her tousled hair back from her face and propped herself up against some pillows, her expression determined. 'As the years went by, my father's tastes...broadened. He started bringing other men home for me to entertain as well, strangers he picked up in bars, or casinos. One night, when we were staying in Monte Carlo, the man he brought home was Lorenzo.'

Brooke's eyes widened.

Francesca just nodded. 'Yes. Now you're beginning to see. Shortly after this incident my father died suddenly, of a stroke, and I inherited all his money. I stupidly thought I could start all over again, put the past behind me and become a new woman. A *decent* woman. I returned to our family home in Milan and set about trying to be one.

'I met Leonardo quite by accident in the street one day. I'd been clothes-shopping and went sprawling on the pavement with all my bags when I tripped over a small dog. Leonardo helped me up and took me for a cup of coffee. We started dating and I thought he was just wonderful. But every time he kissed me I was afraid; afraid to go further; afraid of what I might do, or reveal about myself. He thought I was shy and innocent, so I let him think it. When he asked me to marry him, I said yes, but resolved to stay out of his bed till after we were safely married. Leonardo was gentleman enough to agree.'

Brooke tried not to think of Leo *so* much in love with Francesca that he'd been prepared to wait till their wedding night. He hadn't been at all that way with her. He hadn't taken no for an answer, right from their first date. She wondered how much that had been to do with genuine passion for her, or fury and frustration at not having pushed the issue with Francesca when he had the chance.

'When Leonardo took me to stay at his family's villa on the weekend of our engagement party,' Francesca went on, 'I could not have foreseen that his brother would be one of the men my father had solicited. On those occasions we never exchanged real names. Unfortunately, Lorenzo recognised me immediately, and didn't waste any time getting me alone. I tried pretending I didn't know what he was talking about, but he wasn't fooled. He blackmailed me into his bed the night of the engagement party, and made sure Leonardo discovered us together. After Leonardo broke our engagement, he forced me to marry *him* instead.'

'But you didn't *have* to marry him,' Brooke said, trying to understand this woman.

Francesca smiled again. This time a sad smile.

'That's the problem. I did. I don't know why. Men like my father and Lorenzo seemed to have this...power...over me. I couldn't say no to them.

Lorenzo used to tell me that the night my father picked him up was the best night of his life, that he'd never forgotten me and couldn't believe it when I turned up at his house as his brother's fiancée. He'd been insane with jealousy till he found out I hadn't done anything with Leonardo. He said he *had* to have me, and he didn't care who got hurt in the bargain. He claimed he loved me, but after our marriage he started bringing home other men, just like my father. He liked watching too...'

Francesca's shoulders sagged, her eyes dropping to the bedclothes. 'I hoped, when he died, I was finally free of all the ugliness. But apparently not. As soon as I was alone I started drinking, then I went out and picked up a creep myself. It seems I've become addicted to that debauched way of life. Maybe I can't live without it. Maybe I need it.'

'That's rubbish!' Brooke said sternly, and Francesca's eyes jerked up. 'You're just mixed up and lonely. A lot of women have one-night stands when they're mixed up and lonely. And you're not *addicted* to that kind of life. You're just conditioned. A good psychiatrist should be able to fix you up. Then, later, a good man. But not *my* good man!' she added firmly.

At this, Leo turned back from the window and their eyes met, his still worried, hers seeing his worry and understanding it. She smiled at him, and slowly he smiled back. A thousand little messages were sent within those smiles. Messages of love and apology, of forgiveness and renewed trust.

Still, Brooke had to admit that Francesca had been dead right. Hearing the truth straight from the horse's mouth, so to speak, had been a lot better than hearing it from Leo.

She would not have believed him so readily. She might have thought he was still lying. But no *woman* would have made up such a horror story, not if she'd set her sights on Leo. For all his worldly experience and sophistication, Leo had a fastidious side to his nature. He hadn't minded Brooke not being a virgin, but that was a long way from a woman having entertained hundreds of men in all sorts of salacious ways.

Privately, Brooke wasn't so sure a psychiatrist *could* solve all Francesca's problems. But it would be a darned good start. Perhaps a *woman* psychiatrist might be a good idea, though. Best not put temptation too close at hand. Francesca was very beautiful, and a man was only a man, after all, even when he was a doctor!

'I think, Francesca,' Brooke continued, 'that what you need is to book into a good clinic with a nice, understanding lady psychiatrist. Leo and I will see to it straight away. Meanwhile, I think you should have a nice, relaxing bath and a change of nightie. I'll send the nurse up to help you, shall I?'

'You're…not angry with Leonardo any more?' Francesca asked warily.

'Not now you've explained everything.'

'He loves *you*,' Francesca choked out. 'Not me. How could he love me after what I did to him? But you…you and the children…they are his life. He told me so, just this morning. He was most unhappy when he called you and your mother said you were sick in bed and couldn't come to the phone. You were worried, weren't you, Leonardo?'

Brooke glanced over at her husband, who nodded. 'Yes, Francesca. Yes, I was very worried.' His gaze met hers and she could see the truth in his eyes.

Brooke felt tears well up at the thought of how close they had come to disaster. But she fought them off. The last thing Francesca needed was for *her* to start crying.

'Well, there's no need for you to worry any more,' Brooke said briskly. 'I'm here, and I believe you. *Both* of you,' she added, swinging a reassuring face back to Francesca. 'Now, Leo and I'll just pop downstairs and send the nurse up...'

'My God, you were impressive up there,' Leo complimented her once the nurse had been despatched upstairs.

They were in the huge main living room, Leo standing at the drinks cabinet, pouring himself a whisky, Brooke sitting on one of the brocade-covered sofas which flanked the marble fireplace. She'd declined a drink, her stomach still churning from all that had happened.

'So sensible,' Leo went on. 'And so strong. I've been having all sorts of trouble trying to get Francesca to see a doctor. And you managed it in five seconds flat. Not just a doctor, either. A clinic, no less! I see now I should have brought you with me in the first place.'

He smiled over at her, and suddenly Brooke's façade of strength crumbled, tears flooding her eyes. She'd forgiven Leo with her head, but her heart was still suffering, her bruised and battered heart.

'Yes, you should have, Leo,' she blurted out. 'You

should have told me everything about Francesca from the word go. And you should have told me you loved me much, much earlier.' With a strangled sob, she buried her face in her hands and wept.

Barely seconds passed before he was sitting beside her and enfolding her shuddering body into his arms, stroking her back and soothing her with softly apologetic words.

'Yes, I *should* have,' he agreed. 'And I'm so sorry I didn't. My only defence is that I'm a man, Brooke. A typically proud, very Italian man. When I arrived in Sydney my ego was still incredibly wounded. I knew nothing of Francesca's or Lorenzo's past history at that time, and I felt betrayed by both of them. It wasn't a feeling I relished, I can tell you. But then suddenly I found myself looking into the most beautiful pair of blue eyes in the world, and they were sparkling at me, sending me the sexiest of messages. So I did what any man would have done in my position.'

'You seduced me,' she sobbed against his chest.

'Ah, Brooke…*now* who's not being strictly honest? I never seduced you. You wanted me as much as I wanted you.'

Brooke thought about that for a few moments, then pulled herself together. By the time she looked up at Leo, a sheepish smile was forming at the corners of her mouth. 'True. I fell in love with you the moment I saw you.'

'And I you, *amore mio*, within the week. No, no, that's no lie,' he insisted, capturing her face between his hands and forcing her to keep looking into his eyes. 'Not in hindsight, anyway. I admit I wasn't capable of recognising my love for you in the beginning. I was still too hurt to appreciate the depth of my feelings. And I was still fancying myself in love with Francesca.'

'Oh...' Her heart and eyes sank, showing how vulnerable she still was to the idea of his having been in love with Francesca whilst he made love to her.

'Hey! I said I *thought* I was still in love with Francesca. The truth was I was *never* in love with her. How could I have been, when I went weeks without making love to her? Do you think I would have been that patient with you, even if you *had* been a virgin? I told you once before I simply *had* to have you. Not because of lust. Because of love!'

Brooke thrilled to the sound of his impassioned words. This was the Leo she'd fallen in love with, her hot-blooded man from Milan with his flashing dark eyes and his all-consuming ardour for her.

'By the time I married you I knew that my so-called love for Francesca had been *nothing* compared to what I felt for you,' he proclaimed passionately. 'When you had Alessandro and I saw you in so much pain I would have offered up my *life*, if it would have lessened your agony. When they put our son in your arms and you smiled down at him, I was so choked up with love for you both I could hardly speak.

'And of course that's been my biggest failing. My inability to say those three little words. I love you. I...love...you,' he repeated, kissing her lips after each word. 'I don't know why I found it so hard. Maybe it's a male thing. We men are strange creatures. But I felt it in my heart, Brooke, and I tried to show you in so many different ways. Remember how after Alessandro was born I couldn't wait to take you home to Lake Como to show you off to my parents? Then, once I got you there, and you were just so warm and wonderful with everyone, I loved you all the more. I couldn't keep my hands off you, remember?'

Brooke's heart contracted. 'Yes…I remember. But to be honest, Leo, after what your mother said I started thinking your extra appetite for sex back then was because you were near Francesca, but couldn't have her. And then this last time, when you stopped making love to me, I thought that was because you *were* having her.'

Leo looked truly aghast, his hands dropping from her face. 'Oh, my God… Oh, Brooke… I promise you that had *nothing* to do with Francesca. I was tired, that's all. Stressed out and worried that Lorenzo's death would change my life. I didn't want my father asking me to go back to Italy. That's why I worked like a dog to make sure I got everything done before we left. The day you saw me here at Francesca's place was the only day I came here. Francesca rang me at the office, crying and saying she was going to tell my parents everything! I had no idea what she was talking about, but she was so hysterical that I went over to her place. It was then she told me the whole sordid story, and I knew that somehow I had to keep it a secret from my parents, especially my father. Lorenzo was the apple of his eye. It would have distressed him greatly to find out his beloved son was so depraved. I didn't tell you because I was ashamed too, ashamed of my brother.

'That's all there was to it, Brooke. I swear to you.

Damn it all, Mamma had no reason to think what she did. I can't understand why she did.'

'Perhaps if you'd told her you no longer loved Francesca at some time it might have been a good idea. Still, in hindsight, perhaps my overhearing that conversation wasn't such a disaster. It made me wake up to myself and stop pretending to be something I wasn't. It made me take stock of our marriage and see things weren't as perfect as I thought they were.'

'*I* thought our marriage was pretty perfect.'

'Did you, Leo? Did you really?'

'In the main. Perhaps not when you pretended in bed.' He smiled a wry smile. 'But things certainly improved in that area once you heard I was a potential adulterer, so maybe I should be grateful to Mamma too. It's ironic, though. I came home that night, after hearing Francesca's horror story, desperate to feel your loving arms around me, only to be told you were sick. Then, when I came into the room and you were lying there, looking so damned beautiful, I had to race into the shower and freeze myself for ages to stop the aching. When I came out and you started touching me, I couldn't believe my good—and bad—luck.'

'I couldn't believe what I felt, either,' she said ruefully.

Leo looked taken aback. 'You mean…you thought…?'

She nodded. 'Uh-huh. I was pretty mad, I can tell you.'

A drily amused light glittered in his dark eyes. 'Try getting mad like that more often.'

'Tell me something, Leo.'

'Anything,' he said sincerely.

'You didn't forget about the ruby necklace, did you?'

Leo sighed. 'No. Not entirely.' He leant forward to scoop up his drink from the coffee table, taking a swig before going on. 'I'd intended to give the necklace to Francesca on our wedding day. When we broke up I couldn't bear to look at it, so I shoved it in the house safe and simply ignored its existence. It was my mother who brought the necklace out on the morning we flew home and told me that it was about time I gave it to you. By then I agreed with her wholeheartedly. In fact, I wished I'd thought of it myself. Remember, I had no idea about what she'd been saying about me and Francesca, or what you'd been thinking. The necklace was just something I could give you to show you my love for you.' His smile was wry. 'We men prefer to *show* our love, rather than speak of it.'

Putting his drink down, he took both her hands in his, rubbing his thumbs softly over her fingers. 'Which is what I've been trying to do lately. *Show* you how much I love you. I am so sorry if you've felt humiliated by anything I suggested, or did. I'll never ask you to do anything like I did the other night ever again. I promise.'

'Oh…' she said, disappointed.

'Unless you want me to, of course,' he added, smiling a wicked smile.

'You're incorrigible.'

'And you're incredibly beautiful.' His hand lifted to stroke her cheek and Brooke's heart turned over.

'Hold me, Leo,' she choked out. 'Just hold me…'

His arms went round her, warm and strong and secure. She laid her head with a sigh against his chest and listened to his heart beating: beating with love for her.

A good man, Francesca had called him.

She was right.

He was a good man, her husband. Her Leo.

EPILOGUE

Five years later.

BROOKE peeked around the corner at the top of the hotel's sweeping staircase, smiling her satisfaction at the swiftly gathering crowd below.

'Happy with the turn-out for this year's collection?' Leo said.

'Very. All the main buyers are there, plus the fashion editors from the biggest and best magazines.' Better still, *this* time they'd all paid their own way.

The previous year—Vince's first showing in Milan after three successful years in Sydney and Tokyo—Orsini's had picked up the tab. But it had been worth it to have the *crème de la crème* of the fashion world gather to see what Vince could do. Leo had been right in that regard. You had to invest money to make money. Last year Vince had been declared an up-and-coming new talent. Now, this year, his talent was standing on its own two feet.

'A triumph, then,' Leo pronounced.

'A foregone conclusion, given the quality and class of Vince's clothes.'

'Ah…I do so like a PR lady who has confidence in her product, as well as the producer. Makes me, as the financial backer of Orsini's, a very happy man. Your mother and Matt arrived yet?'

182

Brooke zeroed in on the spot in the front row reserved for special guests. And there they were, the newly weds, holding hands like teenagers. It had taken both of them quite a while to get over their phobias about marriage. Brooke had taken them to task after they'd been living together for nearly five years and told them that was long enough of a trial, and it was time they went for the *real* thing.

'Yes,' she said happily, on spotting them. 'And they both look a million dollars.'

'Who looks a million dollars?' Vince piped up as he hurried past.

'My mother and Matt,' Brooke called after him.

'Well, naturally,' Vince tossed over his shoulder with a florid wave. 'They're both dressed by Orsini. They're two of my best customers.'

Brooke laughed. 'Vince tells everyone who buys anything in his salons the same thing,' she informed Leo. 'Mum and Matt couldn't *afford* to be his best customers, now that he's Europe's latest most *in* designer. The prices on his designer range are wicked.'

'True. I hear Francesca spends a fortune on them every season.'

'Oh, she does. But then Francesca spends a fortune on everything since she met Carlo.'

'The man's a gigolo, if ever I saw one.'

'He probably is, Leo. But he makes Francesca happy. And he doesn't care about her past.'

'That's because all he cares about is her money!'

'Don't complain. He's a regular on Vince's ten best customers list. Not that *you* should talk, husband mine,' Brooke added, running an admiring eye over her superbly suited husband. 'You've been spending a little in that department.'

'I buy his ready-to-wear. Unlike yourself,' he returned drily. 'If I'm not mistaken that saucy little red silk number you're wearing tonight is an Orsini original.'

'A perk of my job,' she defended haughtily. 'Besides, I wanted to wear my necklace,' she added, touching her most treasured possession and trying not to smile too knowingly.

If only Leo knew…

But she didn't dare tell him. Not yet…

'I commissioned Vince to come up with something especially suited to the occasion,' she said silkily.

'He surpassed himself,' Leo complimented, his gaze drifting down the deep V halter-neckline. 'What a pity we have to go to the after-show party,' he added, his eyes telling her exactly what he was thinking. 'It's going to be almost breakfast by the time we get home to Lake Como.'

'I don't think we need to stay *that* long,' she said. 'But I'm not missing this party for worlds.'

It was just after one-thirty and everything was still in full swing when Brooke tapped Leo on the shoulder. 'The car I ordered is here,' she whispered in his ear.

'Car? What car? I thought it was my turn to drive…'

'Just come along, Leo, and don't argue. Your car will be quite safe in the hotel car park.'

She led a confused Leo from the hotel ballroom and down to where a black stretch limousine with heavily tinted windows waited at the kerb.

'If I'd known there was a hired chariot taking us

back to Lake Como,' he complained, scowling, 'I'd have had a few more drinks.'

'Which is exactly why I didn't tell you,' Brooke said as she steered her disgruntled husband into the plushly upholstered interior. 'I wanted you sober and able.'

He sat, smiling now, in the middle of the long back seat, while she climbed in after him and perched on the equally spacious seat opposite. From there, Brooke leant over and whispered her instructions in Italian to the driver.

Immediately the car moved off, and an opaque screen started sliding up behind her, blocking all view of the driver and the way ahead. Leo's eyebrows arched and he threw his wife an amused look.

'You planned all this?'

'Right down to the dress,' she returned, and pushed a button beside her. A bar slid out, well stocked with chilled champagne and crystal glasses.

'Why don't you pour us both a glass, Leo? It's going to be some time before we reach Lake Como. The driver's taking the long way home.'

A devilish gleam fired his black eyes, but he did as he was told. 'What did you mean by right down to the dress?'

'It's very well lined,' she said coolly, although inside she was far from cool. She'd been thinking about this moment all evening, and the excitement of anticipation was bubbling along her veins with more fizz than the champagne.

'So?'

'So no one could see what was underneath it. Or *not* underneath it, as was the case this time.'

'Happy tenth anniversary, darling,' she said seductively as her hand plucked the soft tie on her right hip undone and the dress fell apart.

'But our anniversary isn't for another three days,' he reminded her.

'Then count this as a dress rehearsal,' she murmured, peeling the dress back off her shoulders and letting it slide to the seat...

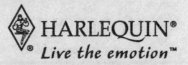

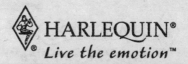

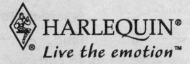

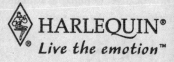

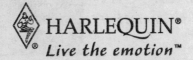